Trouble in Prospect Valley

Kingsley Madsen goes to Prospect Valley to search for gold, but ends up feuding with his fellow prospectors. Before long an argument gets out of hand, leaving one man dead and another man badly wounded. Kingsley is blamed for the incident and after spending seven years in jail he never wants to hear about Prospect Valley again. Unfortunately, other people have plans for him and he has to return to the place where his life had taken a disastrous turn.

When Kingsley learns the truth about what really happened there seven years ago, he must once again resolve the situation at the end of a gun, except this time only the guilty will suffer the consequences.

By the same author

Ambush in Dust Creek
Silver Gulch Feud
Blood Gold
Golden Sundown
Clearwater Justice
Hellfire
Escape from Fort Benton
Return to Black Rock
The Man They Couldn't Hang
Last Stage to Lonesome
McGuire, Manhunter
Raiders of the Mission San Juan
Coltaine's Revenge
Stand-off at Copper Town
Siege at Hope Wells
The Sons of Casey O'Donnell
Ride the Savage River
High Noon in Snake Ridge
The Land of Lost Dreams
The Honour of the Badge
The Hangrope Posse
Shot to Hell
Reckoning at El Dorado
Long Trail to Nirvana
To the Death
The Man Who Shot Jesse Sawyer
Bad Blood at Harlow's Bend

Trouble in Prospect Valley

Scott Connor

A Black Horse Western

ROBERT HALE

© Scott Connor 2019
First published in Great Britain 2019

ISBN 978-0-7198-3063-1

The Crowood Press
The Stable Block
Crowood Lane
Ramsbury
Marlborough
Wiltshire SN8 2HR

www.bhwesterns.com

Robert Hale is an imprint
of The Crowood Press

Typeset by
Derek Doyle & Associates, Shaw Heath
Printed and bound in Great Britain by
4Bind Ltd, Stevenage, SG1 2XT

CHAPTER 1

'Hard Ridge is five miles that way,' the guard said, pointing along the rail tracks. 'I reckon you should go the other way.'

Kingsley Madsen jumped down from the back of the open wagon. The other two prisoners who had been released that morning, Walter and Jack, followed him down. The three men stood in a line and awaited further orders, but none were forthcoming. Instead, with a holler and a crack of the reins the guard hurried the wagon on.

Kingsley had spent the last seven years dreaming about this moment. He'd thought his first taste of freedom would make him so ecstatic he'd run around and holler at the top of his voice until he was exhausted and hoarse, but he felt only lethargic and uncertain about what to do next.

For several minutes the three men watched the wagon head back towards Hard Ridge jail before they turned to each other. Kingsley had never spoken to either Walter or Jack before, but they must have heard about him as they eyed him cautiously while shuffling away.

'I reckon I'll follow that order,' Jack said, breaking the silence.

'But it's a four-day walk to Creighton's Pass,' Walter said.

'Yeah, but I made enemies in Hard Ridge.' Jack turned to Walter. 'What are you going to do?'

'My brother is meeting me a few miles on.' Walter rubbed his jaw. 'He'll have a wagon so we can take you some of the way to Creighton's Pass.'

The offer made Jack smile. Then both men looked at Kingsley.

Kingsley reckoned he might face the problem that had worried Jack, but a desire to spend time on his own overcame him and he shook his head.

'I'll head into town and wait for the next train,' he said.

Walter and Jack murmured in relief, and they didn't wait to see if he changed his mind before bustling away along the rail tracks. Kingsley watched them, and noted that they looked over their shoulders several times. Figuring this type of attitude was a taste of what he might experience in town, he moved on.

He walked slowly, being neither eager to reach his first destination nor sure about what he would do while he waited to ride the rails. The rail tracks skirted along the bottom of the ridge that gave the town its name, and he'd covered most of the journey when he noticed the first people he'd seen since he'd left the other ex-prisoners.

Two men were standing on a high point along the ridge. They were several hundred yards away, but Kingsley reckoned they were looking in his direction. He moved away from them. He walked purposefully now, figuring that if they were looking for him, his best chance of avoiding a confrontation was to reach town quickly.

A few minutes later the men set off down the ridge, but the town then appeared ahead so they wouldn't have enough time to intercept him. When he approached the first buildings on the outskirts of town he glanced over his shoulder and saw they had reached ground level and were following him.

Kingsley maintained his brisk pace, and after passing the first building he turned down an alley. Only then did he break into a run.

He slipped round the back of the next building and scurried on. He hadn't been in Hard Ridge for seven years and the town had grown, but the station would still be on this side of town, which meant he could reach it without returning to the main drag.

Even better, when he returned to the tracks and could see the station, two men were on the platform and seemingly waiting for a train. He stopped running and walked tall so he wouldn't look like a man who was fleeing from trouble.

When he reached the platform he stood between the men and leaned back against the station house wall. He took shallow breaths and after a few minutes he relaxed enough to look around.

His pursuers weren't visible, but as the station was an obvious place for him to have gone, they would probably look for him there. His best hope was for a train to arrive before they came, so he turned to the nearest man to ask him when the next train was due. The question died on his lips.

The man was already looking at him, his sly expression suggesting he wasn't waiting for a train, and the only thing he had been waiting for was him. Then rapid footfalls sounded behind Kingsley as the second man moved closer.

Kingsley jerked to the side, giving the impression he planned to run across the platform. When the two men moved to cut off his escape route he jabbed in a heel and swirled round.

He scooted along beside the wall to reach the corner of the station house and leave his pursuers trailing in his wake. He put a hand to the corner and swung round to head down the side of the building, but then stopped.

His original two followers were walking towards him. The men gloated as they enjoyed their apparent victory, letting Kingsley learn that the men who had followed him were Vandyke and Larry, while the men who had been waiting at the station were Rex and Halford.

'We're pleased you came here,' Vandyke said with a smirk. 'The station is where we wanted you to go.'

Kingsley snarled in frustration and moved to return to the platform, but Rex and Halford had already blocked his path. Rex then advanced on him and slapped a hand on his shoulder, while Halford grabbed him around the chest. They pushed him back against the wall. While they held him securely Larry hurried away and Vandyke faced him.

With time to consider his opponents more thoroughly Kingsley was now sure he'd never met any of them before, so he doubted they had a personal grudge against him. Instead, they were all rough clad and hard faced, suggesting they had been hired to deal with him.

'What do you want with me?' Kingsley asked

9

Vandyke, the apparent leader.

'You're not popular here,' Vandyke said.

Kingsley nodded, with one question answered.

'Who sent you?'

'Friedmann Jacobson wants to see you again.' Vandyke looked Kingsley over. 'But I reckon you were expecting someone else.'

'I was expecting Skelton Pyle, of course.'

Vandyke chuckled. 'Skelton can have whatever's left after Friedmann's finished with you.'

When Kingsley didn't respond to the taunt they walked him round to the front of the building where Larry was drawing up an open wagon.

They bundled him on to the back of the wagon. The few people who were outside weren't paying them any attention, so he didn't struggle.

Vandyke ordered him to lie on his side on the base and keep his head down. He and Rex sat on boxes from where they glared at him, while Halford hurried to the driver's seat.

Larry took the wagon through town. Nobody told Kingsley where they were going and he didn't ask, figuring that no answer would be welcome.

As it turned out, the wagon had trundled along for only a few minutes when it lurched to a halt. Kingsley was ensuring he looked resigned to his fate in the hope that they might relax their guard, so he mustered only

10

a shrug when Vandyke got his attention and pointed.

'We're there,' he said. 'Get out.'

Vandyke waited. When Kingsley didn't move, he nudged his side with the toe of his boot. This time Kingsley sat up and saw that they had stopped a short distance beyond the edge of town, although numerous people were milling around nearby. They were all looking elsewhere, so he turned in the other direction.

A derelict stable was before him, with another ramshackle building beside it that used to be a saloon. With a start, Kingsley recognized the establishment as being the Long Trail saloon.

This place held bad memories for Kingsley. It was in this saloon that he, Friedmann Jacobson, Skelton Pyle and Bruce Russell had enjoyed a last glass of liquor before they had embarked on their ill-fated expedition to Prospect Valley.

Larry and Halford jumped down and took up defensive positions between the wagon and the derelict buildings. Vandyke and Rex pointed, signifying he should join them in jumping down.

Kingsley flexed his shoulders and prepared to take his chances. Then he shuffled along the wagon. He moved slowly, so when Vandyke vaulted over the tailboard, Rex reached for his arm.

Kingsley jerked his arm away. As Rex's fingers

closed on air, he spun round and delivered a flat-handed blow to the underside of his opponent's chin that cracked his head back and made him topple backwards over the side of the wagon.

Kingsley then turned on his heels and jumped off the wagon on the opposite side to his captors. Ahead was open ground, and the people who were wandering around were a hundred yards away, but he hit the hardpan heavily. A foot landed in a wheel rut, pitching him forwards. With his arms wheeling and cursing under his breath, he stumbled for several paces before he was able to right himself and then break into a run – but his chance had already gone.

'One more step and it'll be your last,' Vandyke said behind him.

Kingsley still put his head down and ran for several paces, but Vandyke blasted off a gunshot, which kicked dirt a few yards ahead of him. With a reluctant groan Kingsley stopped.

The noise gathered the people's attention, but now he could see they were unlikely to get involved in his situation. They were standing near a circle of covered wagons, and they appeared to be home-steaders who had stopped on the outskirts of town during a break in their journey.

This hint of trouble made them scurry behind the

wagons. Within moments he no longer had any witnesses, so he turned round and raised his hands.

'If you gun me down someone from that wagon train will report it,' he said, with as much confidence as he could muster.

'I doubt it,' Vandyke said. 'They have no interest in Hard Ridge's affairs, and they're leaving shortly.'

Vandyke gestured with his gun, signifying the saloon. Kingsley sighed, and with his head held high he walked past his captors. When they filed in behind him he carried on into the saloon. Only one man was in the saloon room, Friedmann Jacobson.

Friedmann was sitting behind the only table in the otherwise empty room with a whiskey bottle and two glasses set before him. As his gaze had already been on the open doorway, Kingsley nodded to him.

'Howdy, Friedmann,' he said, receiving a gesture inviting him to sit opposite him.

'Howdy, Kingsley,' Friedmann said when Kingsley joined him at the table. 'As you've seen, I've been planning for this meeting for some time.'

'I've been detained elsewhere for the last seven years, but I gather from your associates' behaviour that you view that as not being punishment enough.'

'I don't, and I'm sure Bruce Russell would agree

13

with me, if you hadn't shot him to hell.'

'I agree, but if I recall what happened between the four of us correctly, you have no reason to threaten me. You didn't take sides, and only Skelton ought to be aggrieved enough to seek me out.'

Friedmann poured a whiskey and swirled the glass.

'You're right, but with a man like you coming out of jail it was wise to act first and find out whether you intend to come after me. I was, after all, the only witness at your trial due to the fact that Skelton was still recovering from the lead you blasted into him.'

'Then I can put your mind at rest. I have no problem with you or with Skelton. I plan to get on the first train and get as far away from Hard Ridge as I can. I'll then put my mistake behind me and find honest work.'

Friedmann sipped his whiskey while he appraised him. Then he put down the glass and nodded.

'I believe you.' He poured a second glass of whiskey, pushed it closer to Kingsley, and stood up. 'Unfortunately, I reckon Skelton might take more convincing than I did.'

'Then while I wait for the train I'll stay out of his way.'

'The next train isn't due for another three days. Worse, by now Skelton should have heard you're

14

here.' Friedmann moved away from the table. 'While you wait for him, enjoy your first whiskey in seven years. I reckon it'll be your last.'

CHAPTER 2

When Friedmann headed to the door, Kingsley picked up his whiskey. He took deep breaths to overcome his concern about Friedmann's chilling warning, and looked around the room. In trying to keep his thoughts from dwelling on what Skelton might have in store for him, he couldn't help but recall how the Long Trail saloon had looked seven years ago on the day his life had taken such a disastrous turn.

All it had taken was for him to make the mistake of answering Bruce Russell's question with another question. . . .

'Would you help out a sixty-niner?' Bruce had asked.

Kingsley had been leaning on the bar, and he appraised a man whose downtrodden expression and slouched posture presented an image of someone who was down on his luck. Kingsley reckoned that image was too exaggerated to be believable, but as he'd been down on his luck a few times himself, he smiled.

'What's a sixty-niner?' he had said.

Bruce introduced himself and sidled closer.

'Sixty-niners are a big part of Hard Ridge's history. I'll tell you everything in return for a whiskey, and I promise you it sure is a memorable tale.'

Kingsley doubted that, but he bought Bruce a drink anyhow. Then to his surprise he spent an enjoyable hour listening to Bruce's story, which also covered the recent history of Hard Ridge.

Twelve years ago the town had been a small settlement that had grown up to meet the advancing railroad. Then everything had changed.

In the spring a gold prospector, Creighton Frost, had returned from Prospect Valley. Creighton had unearthed a nugget that was so big he would never have to scramble around in the dirt again.

Within weeks the news spread about Creighton's discovery, and over the long summer hundreds of men descended on Hard Ridge, from where they embarked on the journey to Prospect Valley. Every one of them was full of hope that they could emulate Creighton's success.

They all failed.

After a frantic six months in which nobody found anything other than a few flecks of gold, and only the merchants in Hard Ridge prospered, the gold rush petered out. The bitter winter that followed destroyed most of the interest in the possibility of more gold being out there, and the town returned to its earlier sleepy state as quickly as it had boomed the previous year.

A few men like Bruce stayed on, hoping they might still get lucky, but one by one they gave up, until now he was the last of them. With the events of that year having faded from most people's memories, and the newcomers caring little about the madness of the short gold rush, Bruce was left trying to raise funds for another expedition.

When Kingsley had listened to Bruce's tale of woe he gifted him a dollar.

'I'm obliged for the tale,' he said with a tip of his hat. Then he set off to seek out a place to sleep that night.

With Kingsley being the only customer who had been prepared to listen to him, Bruce followed him. As Kingsley tramped down the main drag, Bruce sidled along beside him.

'Now that you've heard what happened here, do you want to join me on another expedition?'

18

'From what I've gathered, joining you would involve me paying for everything.'

'That's true, but we'll make a great team. You have the money and I'm the only man in town who knows where Creighton Frost dug up the original nugget. I'm sure that with one more expedition I'll find gold.'

Bruce peered at him with misguided hope in his eyes, so Kingsley resolved to tell him the truth that he couldn't finance an expedition even if he wanted to. He had come to Hard Ridge in the hope of finding work, but as he'd failed to find any, he could only just afford the train fare to the next town.

Kingsley was still trying to find the right words that would inevitably dash Bruce's hopes when he espied an altercation going on beside a nearby hotel. In the shadows, two thick-set men were squaring up to a smaller man, while another man lay on the ground at his feet, seemingly having been knocked down already.

When Bruce saw what had caught Kingsley's attention, he set off towards the hotel.

'What's going on here?' he demanded.

Kingsley reckoned that all Bruce would achieve by getting involved was to receive a beating of his own, so with a sigh he hurried after him.

'Yeah, what's this all about?' he called.

19

The two larger men looked past their opponent. With worried glances at each other they appeared to accept that they were now outnumbered, so they turned around and scampered back along the side of the hotel.

As it now looked as if they had already done enough to stop the fight, Bruce and Kingsley speeded up. By the time they reached the scene of the altercation, the fleeing men had melted into the evening gloom, and they faced a grateful man who introduced himself as Friedmann Jacobson.

'This man is Skelton Pyle,' he said, indicating the man on the ground, who was now sitting up and rubbing his cheek ruefully.

Kingsley nodded. 'I saw you two playing poker in the Long Trail saloon earlier this evening.'

Friedmann smiled. 'I was playing. Skelton was winning.'

'That explains what happened,' Bruce said. 'Those two varmints are the Walcott brothers. They look out for easy targets.'

Everyone nodded and looked at Skelton, who got to his feet and considered the three men with a smile, which made him wince because it hurt his split lip.

'And I'd have lost my winnings if you three hadn't helped me,' he said.

'Me and Bruce didn't do nothing,' Kingsley said. 'It was Friedmann who was taking on the brothers single-handedly.'

'Except I was losing that fight,' Friedmann said. 'Then you two appeared.'

Everyone nodded again as they accepted that no matter who had acted in the most selfless way, between them they had saved Skelton. With the end to this encounter being successful, Kingsley was about to walk away, but Skelton raised a hand.

'Let me show you how grateful I am,' he said. 'I have a large bottle of whiskey in my room at the hotel, which could do with being drunk tonight.'

His offer provoked supportive grunts, so they headed off to Skelton's room to enjoy a companionable evening. Before long they got to swapping stories about their reasons for being in Hard Ridge.

Bruce didn't get to relate his tale, as Friedmann and Skelton had been in town for long enough to have overheard it, but as it turned out they both had similar tales to Kingsley's. They were looking for work, but they'd failed to find any, and were now thinking about leaving town.

Later, with the camaraderie between them growing as the amount of whiskey in the bottle diminished, Bruce made the pitch that Kingsley had been expecting all evening.

'We four have a lot in common,' he declared. 'I reckon we should join forces and get rich together.'

Kingsley licked his lips and looked at the other two men, anticipating their inevitable scoffing, but to his surprise Friedmann and Skelton only shrugged.

'Are you talking about heading to Prospect Valley to look for gold?' Friedmann asked.

'I sure am,' Bruce said. 'I know where Creighton Frost found the nugget. It's just a matter of time before I find one that's just as big.'

'I'm sure you will and I'd gladly join you, but I can't afford to. After that poker game, I'm down to my last few dollars.'

Friedmann looked at Kingsley, who gave a sorry shake of the head.

'I'm sorry, Bruce, but I have the same problem,' he said. 'I have to find work soon or I'll be forced to do what you do and hustle for drinks off strangers in saloons.'

Bruce lowered his head and silence reigned for a while until Skelton spoke up.

'You three men may not have any money, but after tonight, I do,' he said.

Kingsley shrugged. 'If you're minded to go to Prospect Valley, I wish you luck.'

'Except I've already had plenty of luck tonight. I won at poker and you three saved me from a

22

beating.' Skelton raised his voice as he warmed to his theme. 'If you hadn't done that, I wouldn't have any money either, so it's only fitting that I use that money to buy us all a stake in an expedition to Prospect Valley.'

'Are you sure?' Friedmann said.

'I've never been more sure of anything. This feels right. We four have met up at a time when one of us has money, another one has valuable knowledge, and the other two deserve a break after helping a man in need.'

Skelton looked around the group, getting a nod from Friedmann and a punching of the air from Bruce before he looked at Kingsley. He knew that his good feeling about the offer was down to the liquor, but Kingsley still raised his glass and smiled widely.

'Here's to getting rich,' he said.

Everyone whooped. Then, as they made short work of the rest of the whiskey, they planned their next actions.

The group's enthusiasm removed the last of Kingsley's misgivings. So two days later, when they had a last drink in the Long Trail saloon before leaving town, he was genuinely thrilled about what the future might bring. As it turned out, it was a ten-day journey to Prospect Valley, and by the time they arrived that enthusiasm had died out.

23

Before he'd come to Hard Ridge, Kingsley had known people who had prospected for gold, and he'd heard that good friends or even family could squabble when they faced the possibility of getting rich. As their group had only come together during a liquor-fuelled evening, the arguments started long before they got even a sniff of gold.

In truth his companions weren't bad company; they were just men with whom Kingsley wouldn't normally spend time.

Bruce was good-natured and had a seemingly endless supply of tales about his prospecting days. Unfortunately they were all the same. That he had searched for gold and failed to find it summed up every story, except he often took an hour to cover these facts. By the time he'd finished, the others were too bored to stop him embarking on another tale.

Friedmann was a quietly spoken man who ought to have been good company, except he was also a practical man with experience of making long journeys and managing complex tasks. So he wasted no time in organizing everyone even when they didn't need supervision, with the result that after a few days his unnecessary orders irritated everyone.

The goodwill Skelton had generated with his magnanimous offer to pay for everything soon evaporated. He took every opportunity to remind

24

everyone he was funding this expedition, and Kingsley reckoned it wouldn't be long before he demanded a larger share of any gold they might find.

For his part, Kingsley's downbeat demeanour once the initial thrill had receded annoyed the others, so by the time they reached Prospect Valley the group was subdued. Thankfully, when they started work the long days of digging exhausted everyone, and for a while that stopped them arguing.

Bruce directed them a short distance down a gulch that led away from Prospect Valley, deeming this to be the right place to dig. Then he left them to work while he roamed around seeking out other areas they could try. Unfortunately, Friedmann spent so much time supervising Kingsley and Skelton that he didn't shift as much earth as the other two men did, leading to festering resentment about who was putting in the most effort.

After two weeks of back-breaking digging, Kingsley decided he'd had enough, and he resolved to return to Hard Ridge the next day. He kept that decision to himself, figuring he'd just leave quietly at first light to avoid the inevitable recriminations that would ensue.

When they'd eaten their evening meal and were sitting around the camp-fire, he settled back against his saddle with his hands behind his head to watch the other three men bicker. That night, Skelton was in a particularly aggrieved mood.

'How long will we have to dig before we get rich?' he asked Bruce.

'I don't know,' Bruce said with a shrug.

'Except you claimed that you knew when I paid for us to come out here.'

Bruce groaned and looked at Kingsley for support, but having made his decision to leave, Kingsley was in no mood to take sides, and he kept quiet. Bruce then looked at Friedmann, but Friedmann returned his gaze sternly, suggesting he'd like to hear his answer, too.

'We have enough supplies for three months and it could take every day of that time, or we could find something tomorrow.'

'As I'm sure you'll be roaming around again tomorrow, if we find something you won't be here to see it happen and we'll be entitled to keep it for ourselves.'

Bruce narrowed his eyes. 'We agreed to split anything we find equally.'

'We agreed to do that based on us all doing an equal amount of work.'

Skelton cast an aggrieved glare at Bruce and then at Friedmann, who grunted in encouragement, before looking at Kingsley. Again Kingsley passed up the opportunity to take sides in the developing argument.

'I'm doing my share,' Bruce said. 'I've found us a good stretch of ground to dig.'

'Except since doing that you've been elsewhere looking for an even better place to dig, so maybe we should rest up until you've found that better place.'

Bruce sighed. 'It's not that simple.'

'Why not?'

Bruce didn't answer immediately, and that didn't surprise Kingsley, as he'd already worked out why Bruce was spending so much time searching. His promise that he knew the spot where Creighton Frost had found the nugget was just another story that contained more wishful thinking than truth. Bruce was just doing what he'd done on every other expedition: he was hoping he'd get lucky and happen across something.

Kingsley couldn't get annoyed about that, as he was only annoyed with himself for getting drawn in by Bruce's tales – but the same couldn't be said for Skelton. Every moment that Bruce failed to answer only made his brow furrow more deeply. Kingsley reckoned that Skelton was going through the same thought process he had gone through, and was now coming to realize they were wasting their time.

'This is the area where the nugget was found,'

Bruce said, after a while. 'Most men who come here head for the river in the valley and pan for gold. They've had no luck, and I reckon that means. . . .'

'You don't know where to look, do you?' Skelton said, getting up on to his haunches.

'Nobody knows where the gold is lying buried until they dig it up. A load could be lying six inches below where I'm sitting, but unless someone digs down for those six inches it'll never be found.'

'Like I said, you don't know where to look.'

'I do,' Bruce said, his low tone sounding as if he was struggling to sound convincing even to himself.

Skelton snarled and leaned back to slip a hand beneath his belongings. When he rocked forward he was holding a six-shooter.

'You've lied to us.' He raised the gun and aimed it at Bruce. 'And I'm not standing for that no longer.'

CHAPTER 3

As Skelton had located his gun quickly, Kingsley reckoned he'd anticipated that this argument would take a bad turn. In case he needed to defend himself, Kingsley settled his weight on to his side so he could reach for his own gun, which was on the other side of the saddle.

With a nervous murmur of concern Bruce raised his hands while Friedmann shook his head.

'That's enough, Skelton,' Friedmann said. 'We're all tired and irritated, but that'll change when we get lucky.'

Skelton sneered. 'We'll never have that luck because Bruce has made fools out of us, and he sure as hell is going to admit that.'

For emphasis Skelton stretched out his gun arm. Bruce winced, but he didn't reply, presumably because Skelton was right and he couldn't explain his activities.

Kingsley still had no intention of getting involved, but Bruce leaned forward looking as if he was thinking about running towards Skelton and assaulting him. With Bruce being unarmed and with Skelton looking angry enough to respond with hot lead, that encounter wouldn't end well, so Kingsley edged his hand towards his gun.

'Skelton, you need to listen to Friedmann,' he said with a weary air. 'Bruce can't make fools out of us because we are already fools.'

'What do you mean?' Skelton said while still glaring at Bruce.

As Skelton wasn't looking his way, Kingsley reached over the saddle and palmed his gun, although he kept it out of sight.

'I mean we were so eager to get rich we didn't consider that this endeavour was sure to end the same way that Bruce's other trips have, as well as the hundreds of expeditions other luckless prospectors have. . . .'

'That doesn't mean we were fools. Bruce promised us this trip would be different.'

'Anyone who believed that deserves what he gets.'

Skelton gestured at Kingsley with his free hand.

'That's easy for you to say. You risked nothing to

come here, but I paid for this expedition.'

Kingsley had only intended to brandish his gun if it looked as if Skelton was about to start shooting, but that comment made a flurry of anger surge through his veins. He raised his gun and aimed it at Skelton.

'I promised myself that if you told me one more time that you'd paid for this trip I wouldn't be answerable for what I did next. I reckon that time has come.'

Skelton glanced at Kingsley from the corner of his eye, but he kept his gun aimed at Bruce.

'I'll deal with you when I've got an answer out of Bruce.'

With the confrontation clearly about to come to a head, Friedmann got to his feet and leapt aside to put the camp-fire between himself and Skelton, while Bruce settled his weight on to his toes and then ran towards Skelton. With his gun arm tensing, Skelton followed Bruce with his gun.

Fearing that Skelton was about to shoot Bruce, Kingsley fired, slamming a shot into Skelton's side and making him topple over on to his back.

As Skelton was still clutching his gun, Kingsley kept his own six-shooter aimed at him, but he had to duck when Bruce reached down to the fire, grabbed the cool end of a burning branch and hurled it at him. Kingsley had no idea why he'd done that, but as the branch flew through the air showering sparks, the anger that had made him confront Skelton still pounded through his veins, and he fired at Bruce.

His shot hit Bruce in the chest and made him keel over on to his side. Kingsley stayed down, but as he hadn't noticed where the branch had landed he swung his gun from side to side, aiming at Bruce and Skelton in turn.

Bruce didn't move and Skelton only groaned in pain. As it looked as if he wouldn't face any more recriminations, he hurried over to Skelton and kicked his gun away before glancing at Bruce, noting with numb detachment the copious blood spreading across his chest.

'Why did Skelton have to go and draw a gun on Bruce?' he asked Friedmann.

'He was angry,' Friedmann said.

Friedmann's nervous tone confirmed he wasn't sure about Kingsley's intentions, so Kingsley lowered his gun and looked Skelton over. The wounded man was breathing shallowly, and Kingsley figured his chances of surviving were better than Bruce's, so he turned to go to Bruce's aid first – but then saw an object swinging towards his face.

He just had time to work out that Friedmann had

gathered up a cooking pan before the utensil crunched into his brow with a dull clang.

The next he knew he was lying on the back of their wagon, and he was being jostled. The night stars were so bright they made his eyes throb with pain and he closed them; when he next opened them it was light and he was no longer moving.

Shuffling was sounding on the wagon so he raised his head. A thudding pain across his forehead made him give up on the attempt, and he looked around using just his eyes.

Friedmann was kneeling down and looking at something. When Kingsley rolled his head to the side he saw that he was checking on Skelton, who was lying on his back beside him.

'How is he?' Kingsley said.

Friedmann flinched and turned to him.

'He's alive, and that's more than can be said for Bruce,' he said. 'I had to leave him unburied back there to save time and give me a chance of saving Skelton.'

'You did the right thing.'

Kingsley tried to get up, but he couldn't move. A glance down showed he been bound around the legs and his arms had been pinned against his chest.

'After what you did to Bruce and Skelton, I nearly left you behind,' Friedmann said. 'If you give me any trouble, I'll tip you off the wagon and leave you.'

'I won't give you any trouble,' Kingsley said and settled down.

Friedmann moved closer and tugged his bonds to confirm they were secure before he returned to checking on Skelton. Then he moved out of sight.

Presently the wagon moved off, and it carried on through a long day and into the night. The next day Friedmann started off early, and afterwards he maintained a furious pace.

In the end he trimmed three days off their journey time back to town, and Skelton needed that time as by then he was feverish and restless.

Kingsley was as good as his word, and on the journey he gave Friedmann no trouble, but Friedmann still handed him over to Marshal Yarborough, who threw him in the jailhouse.

Kingsley reckoned that once the marshal had heard all the facts he would dismiss the incident as being a falling-out between failed prospectors – something that must have happened many times before – in which everyone was equally to blame for the tragic conclusion. As it turned out, the marshal took the matter seriously, and he was held in a cell for a month until a trial could be held.

By then Skelton was recovering, although he wasn't fit enough to testify in person, but Kingsley was still confident he wouldn't face any problems.

His concerns started when Skelton's testimony was read out in court, as it provided a biased account that downplayed his own aggressive behaviour and made Kingsley the main instigator of the fight. Thankfully, Friedmann spoke about the incident in an impartial manner, stating that Skelton started the argument while Kingsley had remained calm until Skelton threatened Bruce.

He described the gunfight, in which Skelton hadn't fired while Kingsley had fired twice, wounding Skelton and killing Bruce. Kingsley's defence rested on the fact that he had shot Skelton to save Bruce, but that contention sounded hollow in the light of what had happened next.

Kingsley accepted he'd been angry and tired of the arguments, and he'd overreacted when Bruce had turned on him, presumably after misconstruing his intentions. But that version of events wouldn't have helped him, as Friedmann finished his testimony with a surprising revelation.

Friedmann stated that Bruce had thrown the burning branch at Skelton, not at Kingsley, and a moment later Kingsley shot him. Kingsley had thought the branch had been heading towards him and he remembered ducking, but when he thought back he could have been mistaken.

It was dark, and it made more sense that Bruce had attacked Skelton, which meant that he, Kingsley, hadn't killed Bruce in self-defence. With that truth revealed, Kingsley made no further attempts to excuse his actions, and considered himself lucky when he was convicted of manslaughter and got only seven years.

Before he was sent to jail, he didn't speak to either Friedmann or Skelton again, although the marshal told him that not all of Skelton's testimony had been read out in court. Skelton had claimed that if the court didn't find him – Kingsley – guilty, he'd extract his own revenge.

Except the court had found him guilty. So now, seven years later, Kingsley saw no reason why Skelton would want to make him suffer. In addition, Friedmann had even less reason to get involved with helping Skelton complete his revenge. Kingsley put down his glass with the whiskey still untouched and stood up.

Friedmann was standing outside. He was looking at the wagon train where people were again wandering around. Vandyke and Rex were flanking Friedmann, and Larry and Halford were watching him through the saloon's only window. As there was no sign of Skelton arriving yet, he headed to the door.

'Why are you doing this, Friedmann?' he asked.

For a long moment Friedmann ignored him before he turned around.

'As I told you, I don't intend to do anything,' he said. 'Your problem is with Skelton.'

'I can accept that, but why are you helping him by keeping me here?'

'You won't know what's been happening in town for the last seven years, but Skelton has been good to me. I saved his life and he was grateful. I've become a successful businessman, and I owe it all to him.' Friedmann smiled grimly. 'Now it's time for me to repay him.'

'If you're helping him to do this, you're not the man I knew seven years ago. Back then you were a decent man and you behaved fairly at my trial.'

Friedmann waved a dismissive hand at him and turned away.

'I don't have to explain myself to you.'

'You don't, but if Skelton has a problem with me, why isn't he here yet?'

Friedmann flinched – clearly this question was more important than Kingsley thought it was. Friedmann then gestured at Larry and Halford.

'Find out where Skelton is,' he demanded. 'I tire of this.'

The two men headed to the wagon, while

Friedmann moved on to watch them leave, presumably so he wouldn't have to speak with Kingsley again. This left only Vandyke and Rex guarding him and they were outside and had their backs to him.

Kingsley reckoned this moment would probably be his best chance to escape. He walked back to the table, making no attempt to disguise his footfalls, and he scraped his chair as he sat down.

He glanced through the doorway. Friedmann was out of sight and Vandyke and Rex were still facing away from him, so he got up quietly and hurried to a door in the far corner of the room.

The door creaked and stuck after he'd opened it only a foot, but the area beyond was open to the elements as the back room had collapsed. He didn't waste time on checking he hadn't been noticed, and slipped outside.

As he'd expected, he faced open ground with no place to hide, confirming why Friedmann hadn't been overly careful about guarding him. Even if his escape remained undiscovered for a while, he could be tracked down easily.

He hurried along the back of the saloon and stopped at the corner closest to the stable. When he peered around the corner he saw the wagon was heading back to town. He scurried to the stable and skirted around the back, but the scene ahead was as

38

unpromising as he had feared.

Since he'd last been there the town appeared to have expanded in other directions, leaving the saloon and stable isolated. The nearest building was over a hundred yards away across open ground, and the main drag that led through town didn't start for another hundred yards after that.

He watched the wagon until it reached the main drag, by which time he'd decided not to make a run for town. Instead, he edged along the side of the stable to an open doorway, and slipped inside.

The interior consisted only of the four walls, with nothing within that would provide him with a place to hide. Even the walls had numerous gaps, so he hurried to the most intact wall beside the doorway and stopped in a position where he could see the area in front of the saloon.

Vandyke and Rex weren't visible, while Friedmann was facing away from him and watching the wagon train, which was now leaving. The lead wagons were trundling away, while the rest were moving into position to follow.

Kingsley cast another look around the stable, this time searching for something he could use as a weapon. Other than tearing a plank of wood from a wall, he couldn't see anything he could use, so he returned to watching Friedmann.

Then an aggrieved voice spoke up to his left.

'He's not in the saloon!' Vandyke shouted. 'He's escaped!'

CHAPTER 4

'He can't have gone far,' Friedmann shouted, swirling round to face the saloon. 'Find him!'

Scurrying footfalls sounded as Vandyke and Rex hurried into the saloon. Friedmann followed them.

Kingsley moved into the stable doorway as Friedmann paced into the saloon, waving his arms and delivering further instructions.

'We've already looked there,' Vandyke shouted, making Kingsley smile.

Clearly Friedmann could still annoy people with his unnecessary orders. If this behaviour annoyed his men as much as it used to annoy Kingsley, it might slow down their search, but he still reckoned that before long he'd be discovered.

His gaze alighted on the wagon train, and in an instant decision he broke into a run. He thrust his head down and pounded across the ground. He didn't look back to check if he'd been seen, figuring that would slow him down, and he covered half the distance to the nearest wagon in a matter of moments.

Most of the settlers were watching the leading wagons. He doubted he'd have enough time before Vandyke and Rex found him to convince these people to help him, but he saw an alternative: behind the covered wagons there was an open wagon that was loaded down with crates, and these might present him with a safe refuge in which to hide, provided he could get on board without being seen.

As he ran he looked at each settler, and none of them showed any sign of being aware he was running towards them. He figured that Friedmann had been right, and these people weren't looking back as they didn't want to get involved in Hard Ridge's affairs. He reached the back of the nearest covered wagon without facing trouble. It had yet to move, so he scooted round it to the other side and turned round.

He could no longer see the stable and saloon. While keeping the wagon between him and the buildings, he walked backwards until he was standing beside the open wagon. Only then did he glance at the driver, who was slouched forward on the seat and peering ahead as he awaited his turn to move on.

42

Kingsley smiled as his luck held, and moved to the tailboard.

He figured he would struggle to get on board quietly, but the wagon lurched into motion. With only a moment to act he grabbed the tailboard and swung himself up and over the top to land on a crate.

He lay on his belly. So much produce was on the back he could see only the driver's hat, but as the man didn't turn round, Kingsley snaked forwards. He found a gap between two crates and lowered himself into it. As he shuffled down, he cast a last look around.

A covered wagon still blocked his view of the buildings, but unlike before, the driver was looking at him. Kingsley ducked down and swung round to sit with his back against a crate.

He couldn't help but wince after coming so close to completing his escape without attracting a witness. He hunched his shoulders and waited for the inevitable cries of alarm that would lead to his discovery – but the wagon trundled along and built up speed.

With every turn of the wheel Kingsley's hopes increased that he had been mistaken. The man could have innocently looked in his direction and he might not have noticed the stowaway, or perhaps he had seen him, but with the wagon train now moving he'd decided not to delay it. Whatever the reason, he didn't mind as long as he put distance between himself and Hard Ridge.

After five minutes without undue alarm he let himself hope that he had escaped, and after another five minutes he raised his head. The wagons were in a line, with his wagon being the last one. The town was some distance away, and he could see no sign of anyone following.

He breathed a sigh of relief, and settled back down. He still expected that Friedmann would work out where he had gone, but as the afternoon wore on he accepted that Friedmann must be investigating other options first, and there could be a delay before he or Skelton came for him.

With that conclusion he put his thoughts to his next move. He doubted he could stay hidden for much longer, and the settlers would surely view his presence with suspicion. That meant his only option was to slip away quietly and make his way to the rail tracks. Then he could walk to the next station to await the train. To that end, he was pleased that the settlers were steering a course near to the tracks, so he decided to try to remain hidden for as long as they maintained that direction.

Sundown was approaching when someone hollered, and the wagons slowed down. Kingsley lay on his back and resolved to stay in that position until darkness fell, but within moments of the wagons drawing up bustling sounded as several people approached him. He hoped they were only planning to unload some of the produce, but they stopped around five feet away from him.

A murmured conversation ensued, followed by creaking as a man clambered up on to the side of the wagon. A shadow fell over the crate beside him, and with a sigh Kingsley looked up into a pair of cold, glaring eyes.

'Get out of there,' the man said.

Moving slowly, Kingsley stood up and then clambered down to stand within a circle of five men. Further away, other settlers had gathered to watch the encounter with concern. The man who had noticed him before they'd set off moved forwards to take the lead in questioning him. He introduced himself as Manville, and Kingsley provided his name.

'I thought you'd seen me,' Kingsley said.

'I couldn't believe anyone would join us,' Manville said. 'So when I thought I saw something move I dismissed it. I'm sorry I was mistaken.'

'There's no need to be sorry. I'm not trouble. I just needed to get away from Hard Ridge.'

Several men snorted in derision, after which

another man spoke up.

'In other words, you're trouble,' he said and then looked Kingsley over with a sneer before gesturing at Manville. 'I said that staying outside Hard Ridge that long would invite disaster, and it has.'

Manville raised a hand. 'Thorndike, I told you we needed a break before moving on to Prospect Valley, and you need to let Kingsley explain himself. All of us have a reason to leave behind our old lives to seek a fresh start in Prospect Town.'

Manville directed a long look at Thorndike until he mustered a reluctant nod. Then everyone turned back to Kingsley.

'Prospect Valley is a good place to go,' Kingsley said, deciding to provide an answer Manville might welcome hearing. 'I went there several years ago, although back then there wasn't a settlement.'

'You prospected for gold?'

'I searched. I didn't find nothing.' Kingsley shrugged. 'But if you folks don't want my company, I'll make my own way afoot.'

'There's no need for you to do that. Anyone is welcome to join my happy band of settlers, even those who want to waste their time looking for gold.'

When Manville's declaration made the rest of the men face him with their open mouths registering their surprise, Thorndike beckoned for Manville to move away with him. Two other men followed, leaving just one man guarding Kingsley.

The group engaged in a muttered debate and Kingsley couldn't hear what they discussed, but there was no mistaking the nature of the argument. Only Manville thought that letting Kingsley stay with them was a good idea, but as Manville appeared to be the wagon master, he was asserting his authority.

Kingsley stood calmly, not minding how this debate ended. All he wanted from this situation was to avoid anyone being so concerned about his reason for hiding with them that they escorted him back to Hard Ridge.

He now reckoned that if they decided he could stay, he would see what options were available for him in Prospect Town. If they decided otherwise, he would set off along the rail tracks and hope for better luck wherever he ended up.

Presently, with much grumbling and irritated arm-waving, the group disbanded. Three men walked past Kingsley, with only Thorndike stopping to glare at him. Thorndike gestured at the man who had stayed behind to guard him.

'Come on, Norwell,' he said. 'Manville said we have to trust him.'

Thorndike and Norwell both snorted their disapproval of this decision before they moved away.

Kingsley watched them leave and then turned to Manville.

'I'm obliged you spoke up for me,' he said. 'But I don't blame them for being suspicious.'

'I'm as suspicious as they are,' Manville said. 'But I also believe in trusting a man until he gives me a reason not to.'

Manville raised an eyebrow, inviting him to offer a fuller explanation for his behaviour. Kingsley reckoned that if he didn't tell the truth it might cause him bigger problems later, so he spread his hands and smiled.

'I left Hard Ridge jail this morning and I wanted to move on before anyone took exception to me.'

'Why were you in jail?'

'I killed a man and wounded another in an argument that got out of hand. I don't want to ever get involved in trouble like that again, so leaving with you seemed like the best way to make a quick and quiet exit.'

Manville tipped back his hat as he thought this through, and then nodded.

'I'm obliged for your honesty, although it doesn't sound as if you're planning to go prospecting.'

'I'm not. You assumed I intended to do that, and the rest started complaining before I could explain myself.'

'I guess that's true.' Manville smiled and gestured for Kingsley to join him in moving on. 'Our decision was that you can stay with us, but any consequences will be on my head.'

'There won't be no consequences,' Kingsley said as they walked towards the rest of the settlers. 'If anyone comes looking for me, I'll leave and not put anyone here in danger.'

'I hope it won't come to that, and as we're being honest with each other I'll admit I only spoke up for you because I wanted to talk with someone who's prospected out here.'

'I'll tell you about my experiences, although you don't sound like someone who approves of men searching for gold.'

'I don't.' Manville stopped and turned to Kingsley. 'That's because I'm Manville Frost, the son of Creighton Frost, the man who first found gold in Prospect Valley.'

CHAPTER 5

'I came this way many years after your father started the gold rush,' Kingsley said the next morning when the wagons started rolling.

'I never expected that you would have met him,' Manville said.

He offered the reins to Kingsley, who smiled as he took them, enjoying this small gesture of acceptance. The previous evening and that morning he had stayed close to Manville. As none of the other settlers had so much as acknowledged him, Manville was the only person to whom he had spoken. They hadn't discussed prospecting yet, suggesting Manville wanted to talk to him in private. Although Manville was heading to Prospect Valley alone, this was the first chance they'd had to talk.

'I doubt there are many people still around who would have spent time with him, despite everything he did for the area.'

'Both good and bad,' Manville said with a heavy tone. 'I can never forgive him for putting the dream of gold ahead of family.'

'I'd have thought he looked for gold to get a better life for his family.'

Manville shook his head. 'Perhaps that was his intention, but I'd have sooner had a father than a nugget of gold. In the end I got neither.'

During their ill-fated expedition Bruce had told Kingsley several tales about Creighton Frost, but he had never mentioned what had happened to him after he'd found the nugget. Kingsley had assumed that Creighton had left Hard Ridge to start his new life as a wealthy, contented man, but Manville's frown suggested otherwise.

'Are you saying he didn't go back home after finding the nugget?'

'No. He left four children and a wife to look for gold, and the first we heard about his success was when a letter arrived informing us he'd been killed in Pine Springs.'

'Someone killed him for the gold?'

'It was worse than that.' Manville leaned to the side to peer around the next wagon at their route

51

ahead as he collected his thoughts. 'He'd squandered it all before he was killed.'

Kingsley blew out his cheeks in surprise. 'That sounds unlikely. I'd heard the nugget was huge.'

'It was. Some years after receiving the news I visited Pine Springs and got a few more details. Apparently he lost all his usual good sense. He gambled, drank, attracted friends both male and female, and became the most popular man in town, but in one wild year he frittered away every cent.'

Kingsley gave a rueful smile. 'I can guess the rest. Once the money dried up, he was no longer popular.'

Manville nodded. 'He ended up hustling for drinks in saloons trying to sell people the story of his success and downfall.'

'A kind of madness overcomes many prospectors even before they find anything, so I'm sure he's not the only one to have lost control after finding gold.' Kingsley sighed. 'And he's probably not the only one to hustle for drinks and to end up dead. Do you know who killed him?'

'When he was gunned down there were no witnesses so nobody was ever charged, but it was rumoured he swindled a partner out of his share of the gold. Nobody knew who that man was, but it was assumed that when he found my father and learnt that the money had gone he killed him in anger. Then he fled back to Prospect Valley.'

'That seems likely, although your father would have been killed around twenty years ago.' Kingsley directed a long look at Manville. 'It's unlikely that after so much time you'll find any answers.'

'It is unlikely, but not impossible.' Manville gestured at the rising land ahead. 'Either way, I wasn't exaggerating when I said Prospect Town is a good place to settle. Whether I find out the truth or not, I reckon I'll be content there.'

Kingsley nodded. Then, with Manville having told his story, he related his own tale.

He talked about his reasons for joining an expedition to search for gold along with his irritation over their failure to find anything. As he felt defensive about his behaviour, he didn't go into detail.

When he reached the part of his story where the argument had erupted, he provided only the basic facts, which added nothing to the version of events he'd already revealed. Hearing about the gunfight made Manville jut his jaw, but when Kingsley summarized his trial, he grunted in apparent approval of Kingsley's decision not to justify his actions.

'I can show you where I went,' Kingsley said when Manville didn't ask for more information. 'I gather I was digging in the same area that your father found his nugget.'

'I'd welcome that, although from what I've gathered, he's still the last one to find anything.'

Kingsley frowned. 'Bearing in mind what happened to him, all those unsuccessful people probably don't know how lucky they were.'

Manville snorted a laugh, and with that they reverted to companionable silence. They were still in a contented mood when the settlers stopped at noon.

Their relaxed demeanours appeared to alleviate some people's concerns about him, and Kingsley was drawn into a discussion about their future route. The railroad hadn't been there when Kingsley had made the journey before, but he remembered enough about the terrain ahead to trace out in the dirt a map of the main features along with the path he'd taken that would move them away from the railroad.

Everyone murmured with approval, but Thorndike stepped forward and scuffed out Kingsley's map with his heel before tracing out a different route that would keep them beside the tracks for another two days.

When Kingsley bristled, Norwell edged closer as he prepared to defend Thorndike's plan. Kingsley squared up to him, but then Manville caught his eye and shook his head, and after taking several calming breaths, Kingsley didn't object.

'Some men enjoy being contrary,' Manville said when they were moving on again. 'Thorndike doesn't speak for everyone here.'

'He and Norwell seem to be the only sour ones in your group.'

'That's right. I reckon everyone else will eventually be friendly with you, but Thorndike will never accept you and Norwell will back him up.'

'I can see that, although I have to wonder if their problem is with me or with you.'

Manville shrugged. 'It's probably both. They're responsible for keeping trouble away so they didn't like it when I insisted we stay outside Hard Ridge for several days.'

'Were you looking for information about your father?'

'Yeah. A businessman called Friedmann Jacobson promised to help me, but that promise didn't amount to anything.'

When Kingsley had talked about his ill-fated expedition he hadn't mentioned names so he tried to avoid reacting, but Manville must have noticed his discomfort as he narrowed his eyes.

'I came here with Friedmann seven years ago,' Kingsley said with a shrug. 'He was one of the men I left Hard Ridge to avoid.'

Manville digested this information with a slow nod.

'I've already learnt more from you than I did from Friedmann, so that's not a problem.'

Kingsley smiled. Then, to avoid further discussion of an uncomfortable subject, he concentrated on steering a straight course, although whenever Manville wasn't looking he glanced back.

He saw no sign of a pursuit, but for the rest of the day he remained pensive, and he was no less concerned the next day. But with each passing day that concern lessened, until, after another three days, he no longer looked back.

The settlers travelled at a slower pace than he had managed on his previous journey and after a week they had covered only half the distance to Prospect Valley.

By this time most of the settlers were speaking with him and only Thorndike and Norwell sought out reasons to disagree with anything he said, so he relaxed and started to hope his problems wouldn't follow him. As a result, he enjoyed the second half of the journey more than the earlier section.

When he caught his first sight of their destination, the buildings of Prospect Town were bright in the late morning sun. The town had sprung up beside the meandering river that ran through the valley.

He couldn't be sure as he'd spent only a short while in the area seven years ago, but he figured it was a half-day's ride away from the gulch where he had gone with Bruce and the others.

The wagons spread out and drew up a mile out of town on elevated land. The settlers called to each other happily as they saw proof that they'd made a good decision in coming to this place.

They made no move to go any further, and the reason became apparent when a delegation rode out of town to greet them. Several men jumped down from the wagons and with a smile to Kingsley, Manville joined them and moved on to take the lead position.

Manville raised a hand in greeting, and one of the approaching men acknowledged him before moving ahead of the other riders. The settlers who had stayed on the wagons all smiled, making it appear that none of them were anxious about this first, crucial meeting.

They had good reason not to be worried. Manville had told him that they had agreed the details with the town beforehand and they'd already been allocated land along with materials to build homes.

Kingsley tried to foster an optimistic feeling as he watched the riders approach, but with a flinch his hopes died. He recognized the lead rider who was now shouting ahead to Manville.

He was Skelton Pyle.

CHAPTER 6

Skelton drew his horse to a halt beside Manville, who leaned out of the saddle to shake his hand before gesturing at the wagons. Skelton looked along the line, receiving numerous friendly waves.

Kingsley didn't detect that his gaze rested on him for any undue length of time. Then again, even if, as Friedmann had promised, Skelton had been waiting for him to leave jail, he had no reason to suspect he would be with these settlers. Strangely, Friedmann had appeared to think that Skelton was in Hard Ridge, and Kingsley doubted he would have come to this place to wait for him.

Kingsley figured these were mysteries for which he didn't require an explanation right now. He hunched down in his seat, and from under a lowered hat watched proceedings.

The first meeting appeared to go well, because after Skelton and Manville had chatted, the men from the two delegations shook hands. With everyone sporting cheery smiles, Skelton gestured at the town and the surrounding land.

Skelton then waved everyone on, making Manville and the others hurry back to their wagons. While they climbed up on to the seats, the riders spread out to form an escort and rode on towards town.

'That went well, then,' Kingsley said when Manville joined him.

'It sure did,' Manville said. 'I hoped we'd been told the truth, but that didn't stop me from worrying that this place wouldn't be as welcoming as I'd been led to believe.'

'I'm pleased for you. Prospect Town looks like a promising town.'

Kingsley rubbed his jaw as he searched for a way to ask about Skelton that wouldn't sound suspicious, but Manville was in such a good mood that he started talking without prompting.

'I'd not heard of Skelton Pyle before, but after spending only a few minutes with him I could tell he's an impressive businessman. He's built up Prospect Town from nothing using his own resources, and he wants the town to keep growing.' Manville smiled. 'So I'm now confident we can all find a new start here.'

As Kingsley didn't trust himself to reply, he smiled and looked ahead at the town. He now had a clear view of the nearest buildings, and they were new and freshly painted. From what he could see of the rest of the settlement, the other buildings were in an equally well-maintained state.

As they had done in Hard Ridge, the settlers drew up outside town. They formed a circle while Skelton and his group stopped beside the first building and waited for them to be ready.

'We're sure to have plenty to do now,' Kingsley said.

He had hoped to set up a request for him to be allocated a task so he could avoid meeting Skelton, but Manville only smiled and jumped down from the wagon. Kingsley stayed where he was and looked for the best place to stay out of sight. As it turned out, the settlers all alighted, leaving Kingsley as the only one still sitting on a wagon. Then Manville joined Skelton and embarked on a round of introductions.

Skelton took his time in talking with each person, and he even chatted with the children. It was clear this process would take some time, so to avoid attracting attention, Kingsley jumped down.

As Skelton appeared determined to meet everyone, he figured his best plan was to join the people who had already met him. These people were now looking down the main drag.

Nobody else from the town had come out to greet them, and they had spread out, making it hard for him to disappear in their midst, but with the people who had yet to meet Skelton dwindling in size Kingsley waited to make his move.

Presently, Skelton reached a large family, and with the children bustling around, he figured nobody would notice him leave. He walked towards the main drag. He was a few paces away from the nearest man and was thinking up a way to suggest they should explore the town when Manville called out behind him.

'You need to talk to someone who's only recently joined us,' he said. 'Come on over, Kingsley.'

Kingsley winced and turned to find that Manville and Skelton were both looking at him. They were fifty yards away and Skelton was smiling, but that smile died when he registered he was looking at the man who had once shot him.

For long moments the two men faced each other. Then Skelton's arm rose to point at him.

'Kingsley Madsen has come to Prospect Town!' he spluttered.

That reaction was enough for Kingsley, and without thinking he turned on his heel and walked away. He had covered only a few paces when he accepted that as he had nowhere to go, acting guiltily had probably not been the best way to behave, but as he'd now committed himself to this action he carried on.

Terse comments sounded behind him as several people demanded to know what was wrong. He didn't hear Skelton's reply, so he looked over his shoulder.

People were crowding around Skelton, while others were watching Kingsley in bemusement. Kingsley wasn't surprised that Thorndike was the first man to make up his mind about what to do, which was to hurry towards him while waving at Norwell to join him.

Within moments a straggling line of men were following them, so Kingsley broke into a run. He searched for somewhere to go to ground, but the townsfolk were now showing an interest in the newcomers.

They moved into the doorways and the sight of a running man being pursued made them turn their heads to watch him go by. Figuring his best option was to get out of town, Kingsley darted to the left to run beside a church.

He reached the far corner of the church and turned to run along the back. To his left was open

ground and ahead another building was being con-
structed.

The workers had downed tools and were moving
towards him, presumably with the intention of going
to meet the newcomers. When his arrival made them
stop, he slowed down.

Trying to give the impression that nothing was
amiss, he raised a hand to greet the nearest man. The
man smiled, but then everyone looked past him as
rapid footfalls pattered around the corner of the
church.

'Stop him!' Thorndike shouted.

Kingsley glanced back. Thorndike and Norwell
were only twenty paces away so he changed direction
and headed for the open ground.

He pounded along for a dozen paces, but the cries
of alarm coming from the pursuing men galvanized
the workers into action. The men at the end peeled
away to intercept him, forcing Kingsley to veer away
as he sought to go around them.

From the corner of his eye he saw Thorndike and
Norwell closing from one side and the workers
closing from the other, so he thrust his head down
and sprinted, his burst of speed letting him evade
both groups. Then he pounded along across flat
ground.

Shouting could be heard as everyone joined forces

to pursue him, and the noise was some distance behind him. With his hopes rising that he might get away he glanced over his shoulder, only to find that Norwell had hurried ahead of the others and he was only yards away.

Norwell took long strides and then leapt forward and grabbed him around the waist. Both men went down.

They went tumbling along until they came to rest with Kingsley lying on his chest and Norwell lying sprawled over his legs. Kingsley kicked Norwell aside and sought to gain his feet, but his opponent grabbed his right leg and dragged him back down.

Kingsley squirmed, and with frantic shakes he managed to knock Norwell's hands off him. He leapt up and found to his horror that Norwell had delayed him for long enough for his pursuers to spread out around him and cut off his escape routes.

Kingsley ran for the largest gap in the circle of men, but two men closed ranks blocking his path and several men stepped up to him from behind. Hands slapped down on his back and shoulders ensuring he couldn't move on.

With a sigh Kingsley raised his hands in a show of surrendering. That didn't stop Thorndike from taking a secure hold of his arms.

His captors conducted a murmured debate, and

Thorndike gained the honour of being the only man holding him. Then he marched him back to town with the other pursuers flanking them.

When they reached the main drag the rest of the settlers had moved into town. They eyed him with concern so Kingsley looked at Manville, but he stayed back. Thorndike hailed Skelton and pointed at Kingsley.

'We have him,' he said. 'He didn't get far with the whole town joining forces to run him down.'

Skelton moved on to stand in front of Kingsley. He looked him up and down and smiled.

'I'm surprised you're here, Kingsley,' he said.

'From your reaction it'd seem you're surprised I'm here, too.'

'I met Friedmann Jacobson in Hard Ridge,' Kingsley said. 'He reckoned you were there, and you had a problem with me.'

'He was wrong on both counts. I've lived in Prospect Town for the last year, and you have nothing to fear from me.'

Kingsley figured he was speaking for the benefit of the watching people, but he didn't mind if it defused the situation.

'I'm relieved,' he said. 'I had no way of knowing how you'd react when you met the man who shot you.'

'To be honest I've wondered that myself. Now that it's happened I know what I want to do.' Skelton looked him in the eye and then held out his hand. 'I want to be your friend.'

CHAPTER 7

With a grunt of disappointment Thorndike released Kingsley. So with a roll of his shoulders Kingsley shook Skelton's hand.

'In that case I apologize for what I did to you,' Kingsley said. 'The situation was fraught, and at the time most of what happened didn't make sense, but that doesn't excuse the fact that I shot you. I served seven years for that mistake, and I deserved my punishment.'

'It didn't make sense because we were all angry,' Skelton said. 'And I remained angry for a long time afterwards, but I now regret how I behaved and I've devoted myself to better things, such as making something good happen here. I hope you'll join me, and together we can make Prospect Town prosper.'

His words sounded like a speech made by a businessman looking after his own interests, but Kingsley still nodded.

'I reckon I'll do that. It's the least I can do for you and for the memory of the man who wasn't so lucky, Bruce Russell.'

Skelton's eyes flickered with an emotion, but he blinked it away before Kingsley could work out what had concerned him. Then he moved away to resume introducing himself to the newcomers.

Kingsley nodded to the people who had helped Thorndike escort him back to town. Skelton's reconciliatory words didn't appear to have swayed them as they looked at him with stern eyes. Then these men moved off to resume their previous work, leaving behind the settlers, who glared at him with the same level of antipathy they'd shown when they'd found him hiding on a wagon. With muttered comments to each other these people then disbanded, leaving only Thorndike and Norwell to stand with him.

'I said you were trouble the moment I first saw you,' Thorndike said. 'Now everyone can see that for themselves.'

'Skelton Pyle says I'm not trouble,' Kingsley said.

'That's because Skelton's a better man than you are. You shot him, and it sounds as if you killed this other man, Bruce Russell.'

69

'You weren't there that day, but I was, and so was Skelton. We don't have a problem with each other.'

'That changes nothing, because I sure have a problem with you.' Thorndike pointed at him. 'I'll be watching you, Kingsley.'

Thorndike raised his chin as he awaited a retort, but Kingsley had tired of talking with him. When it became clear he would remain silent, Thorndike and Norwell both sneered at him before they headed off to join Skelton's group, leaving Kingsley standing alone.

Manville had clearly been waiting for Thorndike and Norwell to leave as he moved on to join him.

'So Skelton was the man you shot,' he said.

Kingsley frowned. 'Yeah. I shot him and killed Bruce Russell. Bruce mainly worked alone, so I doubt anyone will be annoyed enough about that to seek me out.'

'In which case you can stop worrying about your past and concentrate on your future.'

Kingsley rubbed his jaw as he tried to foster a more optimistic mood and then nodded.

'I will, and I can start by helping you deal with your past. Whenever you're ready we can visit the place where your father made his discovery.'

Manville looked at the settlers, who were still eyeing them with undisguised hostility. He pointed out of town.

'There's no reason to delay, while there are plenty of reasons for you to be elsewhere right now.'

As Kingsley reckoned Manville was right that he should give everyone a chance to cool down, he joined him in heading back to Manville's wagon. On the way Skelton broke off from his introductions to glance at him and then talk with Thorndike.

When Thorndike moved away he was smiling. This hint that Kingsley's problem with Skelton might not be as resolved as he had hoped it was, ensured that he wasted no time in climbing on to the wagon and taking it away from Prospect Town.

With him not trusting Skelton's magnanimous attitude, he couldn't help but wonder what his real intentions were, as well as the reason for Friedmann's mistake about his whereabouts in Hard Ridge. He couldn't come up with any answers, and before long the more immediate concern of finding the place where he had camped out seven years ago took over his thoughts.

He remembered that Bruce had directed them along Prospect Valley, and they had stopped in a gulch that headed to the west. He couldn't recall any landmarks prior to them reaching this spot, but he still looked for terrain that he recognized.

Manville was quiet and lost in his own thoughts. So

as the afternoon wore on without him spotting anything that looked familiar, Kingsley didn't have to try to appear more confident than he felt.

Sundown was around two hours away when, with a sigh of relief, he saw the entrance to the gulch a few miles ahead, its appearance bringing up an old memory of Bruce stopping to point out their destination.

He smiled and turned to report the good news to Manville, but Manville was gnawing at his bottom lip with his eyes distant. Kingsley had to lean forward and cough to get his attention.

'We'll be in the right area before dark,' he said and then pointed at the gulch.

'Good,' Manville said. 'When we get there will there be somewhere safe for us to hole up?'

Kingsley frowned, and when Manville looked around the side of the wagon, he glanced back.

'Are we being followed?'

'I reckon so. I've caught sight of riders behind us several times, and they're the first travellers I've seen since leaving Hard Ridge.'

'That doesn't have to mean trouble. This is the area where most prospectors went. Even after another seven years without anyone finding anything, I'm sure people still come here hoping to get lucky.'

72

Manville shrugged, not appearing heartened by Kingsley's theory, so Kingsley urged the horses to speed up. As they approached the gulch, Kingsley tried to recall more details about the area.

He remembered how one day Bruce had left them to scout around, and the other three men had been curious to see where he went. They had followed him out of the gulch and into a narrow and winding pass that led away from Prospect Valley and which had been hidden from view until they were almost upon it.

They had gone to a point where the sheer rock sides closed in until they were effectively riding along a fissure. The space was only wide enough for the three men to ride beside each other with gaps between them of just a few feet. The rock walls to either side had started to feel oppressive when they had ridden around a bend and found Bruce standing there waiting to be discovered. There had followed another of the arguments that had blighted the expedition, but the memory helped Kingsley to decide what they should do next. He moved away from the river, but when they reached the entrance to the gulch he carried on.

Manville shot a bemused look at him, but then smiled.

'You reckon that if the riders head into the gulch,

they're probably not following us.'

'And if they don't go there, I know of a place a few miles on where we can hole up.'

This declaration made Manville sigh with relief, and Kingsley relaxed when he looked back and the lie of the land blocked the view of the area behind them. Kingsley still maintained his speed until they approached a massive angular boulder that he remembered as being at the entrance to the pass.

He slowed down and with a glance back down the valley, they headed into the pass. His memory turned out to be accurate, and within moments they reached a bend that would let them remain out of the sight of anyone who rode by.

Kingsley stopped the wagon. Without discussion Manville clambered into the back of the wagon and returned with two six-shooters. They jumped down and headed back to the entrance.

'The ground's soft and we've left a trail for the riders to follow,' Manville said as he peered at the nearby terrain.

'We have enough time to swipe the wheel ruts away,' Kingsley said. 'But I'd prefer to leave them. How the men react when they see the tracks heading this way will prove what they're doing.'

'I hope the answer is that they do nothing.' Manville hefted the six-shooter on his palm. 'But if they're planning to give us trouble, I reckon we should give it to them first.'

Kingsley nodded and they clambered up the boulder to lie on the top. They settled down in an area where a raised length of rock protected them from being seen from down the valley. In this position they wouldn't be able to see the approaching riders, but they could watch the men ride away.

Fifteen minutes passed quietly. Then the clop of hoofs sounded nearby. The hoofbeats came closer and then receded, before again heading towards them, giving the impression that the riders were looking for them, but they were unsure about where they had gone.

Kingsley and Manville exchanged nods and moved towards the edge of the boulder. They lay on their bellies in a position where the men would ride by below them if they tried to follow them into the pass.

Presently, a murmured cry of triumph sounded, followed by an affirmative grunt. Then the hoofbeats clumped with an insistent rhythm as the riders hurried towards them.

'Two men,' Kingsley whispered.

'Two?' Manville said with a furrowed brow.

Kingsley didn't have time to question Manville about what had confused him as the riders came into view. They were only ten yards away from the entrance, and from his elevated position he couldn't see their faces, so they were unlikely to notice him, but he recognized the men's clothing.

He had intended to stay on the boulder and demand answers at the end of a gun, but the sight of Thorndike and Norwell made him snarl with anger. He raised himself, making Manville shoot a worried look at him, but when he saw his intention he gestured, indicating he'd take on the trailing rider, Norwell.

Kingsley waited until Thorndike passed below him. Then, with a glance at Manville to coordinate their actions, he leapt down from the boulder. He fell for a brief moment before slamming down on Thorndike's back, unseating him. The two men went tumbling.

Kingsley executed his leap well and landed feet first in the soft dirt before he toppled over, but Thorndike went sprawling on to his back and then lay winded with his arms and legs spread wide apart. Kingsley leapt to his feet and hurried over to him.

He dragged Thorndike to his feet, leaving him hunched over. He punched his stomach making him groan, and hammered a round-armed punch into his jaw that sent him stumbling backwards into the boulder. Thorndike cracked the back of his head against the rock and slid down to the ground, so

Kingsley turned away to see how Manville was faring.

Manville had knocked Norwell from his horse, but Norwell had fought back and the two men were wrestling with each other. Norwell had slapped his hands on Manville's shoulders while Manville had done the same to Norwell, and both men were trying to tip each other over. Kingsley hurried over to them and grabbed Norwell's upper arm.

He yanked Norwell backwards, drawing him clear of Manville's clutches, but Norwell swung round and launched a scything punch at Kingsley's face. Kingsley ducked, letting the intended blow whistle over his back, and then stepped forwards to slam his shoulders into Norwell's stomach. He drove forwards, then raised himself to tip Norwell over his back. Norwell somersaulted before crashing down on the ground, where with a groan he moved to raise himself – but Manville was already on him.

Manville knelt down on Norwell's chest and drew back his fist, but he only shook his head with a warning not to retaliate, so Norwell went limp. With him subdued, Kingsley turned away to find that Thorndike was sitting at the base of the boulder and peering at him groggily.

'Explain yourself,' Kingsley demanded.

'I'm not saying nothing to you,' Thorndike said, while fingering the back of his head and wincing.

'Then I'll just have to knock your head against that boulder until you start talking.' Kingsley advanced a pace on Thorndike, and that was enough for the fellow to raise a hand in a gesture to ward off Kingsley.

'There's nothing to tell you. We just wanted to see what trouble you were causing out here.'

Kingsley shrugged and stepped up to Thorndike. He dragged him up from the ground and pinned him back against the boulder.

'You know that Manville wants to find out everything he can about his father's activities.' Kingsley drew Thorndike forward and then slammed him back against the rock for emphasis. 'Why should that interest you?'

Thorndike glared at him in defiance, so Kingsley shook him again and this time Thorndike's head clunked back against the rock. Thorndike grunted in pain and slumped down.

'It doesn't,' he murmured with a defeated tone. 'But Skelton was worried about what you might be doing, so we offered to find out what we could.'

'So the man who told everyone he wants to be my friend is worried.' Kingsley glanced at Manville, who frowned. He turned back to Thorndike. 'Go back to Prospect Town and tell Skelton that I really don't have a problem with him, but if he keeps checking up on me, I will have one.'

Thorndike nodded and raised a hand to rub the back of his head. Kingsley drew him forwards and shoved him towards Manville and Norwell.

Thorndike stumbled on for a few paces, but when he came to a halt he stood up straight. Then he turned to glare at Kingsley with some of his usual truculence returning.

He beckoned for Norwell to join him and when Manville dragged his captive to his feet and pushed him away the two men headed to their horses. When they'd mounted up both men sneered at them, but they didn't offer any final threats.

Kingsley and Manville stood together to watch them ride away.

'I reckon they will go back to Prospect Town,' Manville said. 'But this isn't over yet.'

'I'm sure you're right. Those two won't try to placate Skelton, and I doubt they'll even mention we bested them, but I'm sure they won't waste a moment before they start turning the rest of the settlers against me.'

'They can't do that. From the expressions on everyone's faces when we left, I'm the only one who's on your side, but I wasn't talking about them.' Manville turned to him and frowned. 'I first saw that we were being followed a few miles out of Prospect

Town, but the problem is: Thorndike and Norwell weren't the men I saw.'

'Are you sure?'

'I reckon there were five men, and they were clad in darker clothing than Thorndike and Manville were wearing.'

'Have you ever seen them before?'

'They were too far away for me to answer that.' Manville sighed. 'So we'll just have to hope they were innocent prospectors.'

Manville directed a long look at him. Then, moving quickly, he headed back to the wagon.

CHAPTER 8

That night Kingsley and Manville stayed in the pass close to the entrance, as they figured it was an ideal place to see off trouble. Despite both men's concern about the intentions of the mystery group of riders, the night passed peacefully.

The next day Kingsley showed Manville around the area, taking him along the side of the river and into the gulch. While both men kept a watchful eye out for the riders, Kingsley talked about his previous expedition there. The familiarity of the surroundings helped him to drag up memories he'd previously forgotten about, and he was able to go into greater detail than before. He also related what he could remember about Bruce's tales of his exploits.

To his surprise he found he was eager to visit the place where they had made camp, so after riding along for a few miles he headed to the base of the steep slope on the southern side of the gulch. He located the right area without any detours, so he found himself standing on the spot where an argument he had tried to ignore, followed by a flash of anger, had led to disaster. When Manville joined him he felt a need to talk through the incident while pointing out everyone's positions and movements.

During his detailing of the confrontation Manville said nothing, and when Kingsley had finished he walked away for a short distance to look at a length of ground that still bore the scars of their digging.

'I've always thought I'd never understand why men want to find gold and become rich quickly,' he said. 'Having seen the unforgiving land they have to dig, and heard about the hard work that's involved, I now know for sure I'll never understand.'

Kingsley snorted a laugh and moved on to join him.

'There are easier ways to become successful,' he said. 'Your father was the exception.'

'He was, and if your group could end up fighting because they didn't find anything, it's even easier to see why someone killed him after he did find something.'

'Does that mean your quest to find answers ends here?'

'I've seen enough of this place, but my quest will end only when I find out who killed him.' Manville sighed and turned away. 'I hold out little hope I'll be able to do that, but I'm in Prospect Valley now. I'm sure to meet other men who have come here to look for gold, and maybe one of them will remember meeting my father or his partner.'

Manville gestured for Kingsley to join him in heading back to the wagon, but when they were on the seat Kingsley headed across the gulch.

'Before we go back to Prospect Town and try to repair whatever damage Thorndike and Norwell are no doubt causing, there's one more place we should go.' Kingsley pointed to the north. 'I've shown you where I was digging, but you haven't had a proper look at the place where I reckon your father found the nugget.'

Manville raised an eyebrow in surprise. 'So why were you digging here when the best chance of finding gold was somewhere else?'

'That's one of the things we argued about. Bruce directed us to dig in the gulch, but he explored elsewhere. At first we accepted that he was acting in all our interests, but we suspected he'd lied to us about the location of your father's find and he wanted to be alone when he found something so he could keep it for himself.'

'He must have been confident of success.' Manville rubbed his chin. 'Did Bruce ever mention he'd met my father?'

'He didn't, and that man sure talked a lot, but he sounded confident he knew where Creighton had gone.'

Manville shrugged. 'As he didn't meet him, all his information would have been second hand.'

Kingsley nodded, then they reverted to silence as they headed out of the gulch and along to the boulder where they'd overcome Thorndike and Norwell. They rode into the pass at a steady pace, but had to slow down when they reached the area where the fissure narrowed. On his previous visit he and the others had turned around after finding Bruce there.

Ahead, the gap between the two walls of rock narrowed even more, leaving the wagon only a few feet of spare space on either side. As they would already struggle to turn the wagon around, he drew up.

'Bruce came this way, but I don't know how much further he went,' he said. 'He referred to this place as a pass, so it must lead to somewhere, but how badly do you want to see what's ahead?'

Manville looked at the sheer rock looming above them on either side. He shook his head as if he was ready to turn back, but then sighed.

'As I don't ever want to come back here, I guess I should see everything I need to this time.'

Manville jumped down and the two men walked on. Kingsley looked at the ground and up the rock faces searching for hints of where prospectors might have chipped away at the rock, but he saw no sign of activity. Presently they moved around a bend and found that the pass widened, but the way ahead was blocked to a height of around a hundred feet as the rock on both sides had collapsed into the fissure.

'Do you want to see what's on the other side?' Kingsley asked.

Manville smiled. 'I'm losing interest rapidly, but I'm just intrigued enough to see if I can climb up.'

Manville moved on, and when he started scaling the mound without difficulty, Kingsley followed him. Five minutes later they reached the summit of the heap of fallen rocks, and were rewarded for their efforts with the sight of the fissure opening up ahead. They clambered down the other side of the mound and walked on.

When they reached open ground, ahead was a broadly rectangular area that was several hundred yards across on its longest side, and surrounded by sheer walls of rock on three sides. Numerous other fissures like the one they had traversed were visible, but their entrances were so narrow that Kingsley reckoned they were probably short and not worth exploring. They headed to the fourth side where the rock had collapsed, creating a mass of angular boulders that abutted against each other.

When they reached the base both men stood with their hands on their hips peering at the confusing tangle of boulders.

'This must be the place that interested Bruce,' Kingsley said. 'Before that, your father probably came here and just got lucky.'

'He probably did, and I can see how lucky he must have been.' Manville tipped back his hat. 'A man could search here for years and still not thoroughly examine every boulder.'

'You're right, and that's only the section we can see. We don't know what's beyond these boulders.'

Manville laughed. 'If that's your way of asking whether I want to climb again, the answer this time is that I've seen enough.'

Kingsley nodded and then cast a last glance at the area before he started to turn away. Then he saw something move.

He turned back. He didn't see the movement again, but he figured it had come from a point near to the top of the boulders.

'Did you see that?' he asked.

'No, but I saw your reaction.' Manville peered up

86

the slope and narrowed his eyes. 'I can see something up there.'

Manville was looking to the left of the place where Kingsley had seen movement. Kingsley followed his gaze and saw a box standing proud on the top of a boulder.

'Have you still seen enough?' he asked.

Manville smiled. Then they clambered up the nearest boulder.

The rocks were larger than on the previous slope they had climbed. Unfortunately they turned out to be harder to traverse as when they reached the end of a boulder it didn't always provide access to the next one leading to them doubling back several times.

After ten minutes they reached the box, finding it was open and filled with rocks.

'These rocks might contain gold, but they just look like rocks to me,' Manville said.

'It's the same for me. Then again, my only attempt at prospecting proved I don't know what I'm looking for.'

Manville picked up a rock and examined it intently.

'Clearly someone thought they were interesting enough to collect.' Manville hefted the rock and then picked up another one and tossed it to Kingsley.

'Take a good look at this one.'

'What am I looking for?'

'I have no idea.' While moving only his eyes Manville glanced to the side. 'But I reckon a man who does know what to look for is hiding over there.'

'Then it looks as if you'll get your first chance to question a prospector.' Kingsley threw the rock into the box. 'As we've strayed into his domain, I suggest we try to avoid raising undue alarm.'

Manville threw down his rock and turned to face two large boulders. These boulders had fallen against each other with a third flat rock lying over them, creating a protected area beneath that was large enough to accommodate a standing man. Several objects were lying within the space in the shadows, suggesting it was being used as a shelter.

'I'm pleased I found you,' Manville called. 'I just want to ask you a few questions.'

Nobody replied, although Kingsley noticed a change in the light level within the shelter as the man moved around.

'That was too alarming,' he whispered from the corner of his mouth. 'You shouldn't have implied you were looking for this man, and you should have just asked your main question.'

Manville nodded and moved a pace closer to the shelter. He spread his hands and raised his voice.

'I want to talk to prospectors about Creighton Frost. I'm Manville Frost, Creighton's son.'

Silence reigned for several moments. Then the man moved, his footfalls scraping across rock.

Manville took another pace forwards, but a gun emerged from around the side of the nearest boulder and the man fired off a couple of blind and wild shots.

Manville scrambled back to join Kingsley, then both men leapt over the box and lay on their bellies on the other side of the sloping boulder in a position where they could no longer be seen.

'I thought I told you to be less alarming,' Kingsley said with a smile.

Manville gestured ahead. 'Please feel free to do better.'

Kingsley raised himself to appraise the shelter. He couldn't work out how he might diffuse the situation, but he didn't need to try, as the gunman spoke up.

'I don't care who you are,' the man shouted, his statement making Kingsley gulp. 'You'll stay away from my haul.'

Manville turned to Kingsley and shrugged before pointing down the slope.

'I guess I got my answer,' he said. 'Not everyone will want to answer my questions and I can't force him to talk.'

Kingsley ignored him and looked aloft as he recalled the gunman's demand. He was sure he hadn't been mistaken, so he shook his head.

'You can go. I have to stay.'

'Why?'

'Because I recognized that man's voice. He's Bruce Russell!'

Manville thought about this for a moment, and then flinched back in surprise.

'And Bruce Russell is the man who. . . ?'

'Yeah.' Kingsley stood up and drew his gun. 'He's the man I killed seven years ago.'

CHAPTER 9

With determined paces Kingsley headed towards the shelter. He didn't speak, figuring that Bruce had probably yet to see who was accompanying Manville.

'I can hear you moving around out there,' Bruce said from within the shelter. 'I will defend myself, so don't come no closer.'

Kingsley stopped twenty feet from the nearest boulder and aimed his gun at the spot where Bruce had been standing when he'd fired at them. For long moments he waited for the fellow to make a move.

Footfalls sounded behind him, and Kingsley waved at Manville to stay back. But Manville kept walking, so Kingsley turned to find that he was beckoning him to return.

Kingsley winked, trying to indicate he wasn't planning to assault Bruce, but when he turned back his

91

opponent edged his gun into view. Before he could fire Kingsley blasted a shot into the rock a few feet above Bruce's hand, making him jerk his gun back out of sight.

'I haven't got nothing worth stealing,' Bruce said. 'I've not had no luck yet.'

'You've had more than enough luck for one lifetime,' Kingsley said, and then walked on. 'But like Manville said, we just want to ask you some questions.'

A gasp of surprise sounded within the shelter. Assuming that Bruce had recognized his voice, Kingsley speeded up. He covered five paces quickly, and then Bruce came into view in the shelter.

He was standing with his back against the side of the boulder with his gun held slackly, presumably as he reeled from the shock of meeting Kingsley again. Kingsley still aimed his gun at him.

'It's you,' Bruce murmured.

'It sure is,' Kingsley said as he advanced on the old prospector.

At the last moment Bruce got over his shock and raised his gun, but Kingsley was on him. He slapped the gun aside, making it go spinning across the shelter, and then shoved Bruce in the side, making him stumble away for a pace.

Bruce stilled himself so Kingsley pushed him

again. This time Bruce fell over and landed on his back. Kingsley loomed up over him with his gun aimed down at his opponent's chest.

'What do you want with me?' Bruce said, his voice high-pitched with worry.

'I reckon you can figure that one out for yourself. I spent seven years in Hard Ridge jail for killing you.'

'You might not have killed me, but you sure shot me.' Bruce pointed at his chest.

'At the time I was trying to save your life.'

'You had a strange way of doing it.'

Kingsley scowled. 'Maybe I did, but right now the only thing on my mind is that I doubt I can get sent back to jail for killing a man I've already killed.'

Kingsley raised his gun and aimed it at Bruce's head, making him gulp, but Manville moved into the shelter and stood to Kingsley's side.

'Quit with the threats, Kingsley,' he said. 'I know you won't take revenge on him.'

'You don't know me well enough to say that.' Kingsley rolled his shoulders, but then with a thin smile he moved the gun aside and softened his voice. 'Just tell me what happened seven years ago, Bruce, and make your explanation a particularly good one.'

Bruce shuffled backwards and sat up. When Kingsley didn't object he got to his feet and faced him.

'I came to lying in our camp with a bullet in me. I was weak and in pain. I called out. Nobody came. As I could only drag myself along for a few yards, I accepted you'd abandoned me and I was doomed to die.'

'Friedmann Jacobson reckoned you were dead, and with Skelton Pyle wounded he resolved to get him to Hard Ridge as quickly as possible.'

'Whatever he claimed, I needed help too, but I was lucky. There was a group of prospectors nearby, and they heard the gunfire and found me. One of them knew some doctoring and fixed me up. It took me weeks to recover, and when I felt better I helped them with their search. We didn't find nothing, so I returned to Hard Ridge.'

Bruce rubbed his jaw and glanced at Manville, who smiled.

'Kingsley is angry, but he won't kill you,' he said. 'He just wants to know what happened.'

'I learnt that Kingsley was in jail for killing me.' Bruce raised his chin and looked Kingsley in the eye. 'Frankly, I figured that was a just punishment. I resolved to keep my survival a secret and head back to Prospect Valley the first chance I got, which is what I did.'

Kingsley tipped back his hat while shaking his head.

'So you've spent the last seven years here?' he said.

'Sure.'

'I find that hard to believe. When I first met you, you didn't have a cent to your name, so how did you raise the money?'

Bruce waved him away and then walked further back into the shelter for a few paces and sat down.

'I've told you what I did seven years ago. What happened after that is my own business, but I'll tell you one thing: I don't regret nothing. I suffered, and I'm glad you did.'

'I'm obliged for your honesty, but it doesn't change the fact I never wanted to harm you.'

Bruce put a hand to his brow and shrugged.

'What with all the pain I suffered afterwards my memory of that night isn't that good, but I can remember some things. All three of you argued, but you were the only one who was angry enough to do any shooting.'

Kingsley moved forwards to stand over Bruce.

'Maybe that's the way you remember it, but the truth is that Skelton was about to shoot you and I shot him to save you. Then I thought you were about to attack me, so I shot you.'

Bruce glared at him while rubbing his chest, presumably fingering his old wound.

'The result still amounts to the same thing. I

nearly died, and it's your fault.'

Kingsley was about to snap back an angry retort, but Bruce's flared eyes suggested this was an argument he wouldn't win, and they were doomed to keep on repeating the same points. He sighed, and backed away for a pace.

'In that case, I apologize.'

Kingsley held out his hand. Bruce looked at it and folded his arms.

'I'll accept your words, but not your hand. Now leave me alone.'

'We can't do that.' Kingsley stepped aside and gestured at Manville. 'You know more than most about Creighton Frost, and Manville would welcome hearing those tales first hand.'

Bruce glanced at Manville, but then looked away.

'Tales is all they were. I never met him.'

'I'll settle for hearing tales,' Manville said, moving forwards to stand with Kingsley. 'I don't know much about my father's life out here, and it'll help to fill in the time while we head back to Prospect Town.'

Bruce raised his eyebrows. 'I'm not going there.'

'You are.' Manville glanced at Kingsley and winked. 'Most of the town reckons Kingsley is a killer, so they'll welcome seeing that the man he's supposed to have killed is alive and well.'

'What will I gain from doing that?'

'Our gratitude.'

Bruce glared at Manville, but when Manville met his gaze he sighed and lowered his head.

'I guess it'd be good to see how much the town has grown recently.' He patted his legs and stood up. 'I'll gather together my equipment and join you.'

Manville nodded, and he and Kingsley left the shelter. Kingsley moved on to stand beside the box of rocks, where he looked down into the open area. Neither man spoke as Kingsley tried to work out whether he felt angry, relieved, or just bemused by the recent development. He was no nearer to an answer when Bruce emerged with a pack hoisted up on to his back. He headed to the box and rearranged the contents.

'I assume they're worthless,' Manville said.

'Sure, but they look enticing enough to distract folk,' Bruce said.

'I'd have thought a distraction would only be useful if you have something valuable you don't want people to notice.'

Bruce shrugged and busied himself with throwing rocks into the box. Manville and Kingsley left him to finish his work and started picking out a way down the slope.

Manville decided on a route and set off in the lead. Kingsley moved to follow him, but then looked over his shoulder at Bruce to check he was ready to leave now.

Bruce had his back to them while he hurled rocks into the box. Then with a quick gesture he pocketed a small rock before glancing Kingsley's way.

Kingsley turned his head away before Bruce could notice his interest, and headed down the slope after Manville.

CHAPTER 10

The three men walked back to the fissure and along it. They started talking only when they reached Manville's wagon, when they debated how to turn it round in the confined space. As it turned out they accomplished the task with a quick manoeuvre. Kingsley then took the reins while Manville sat beside him, and Bruce sat in the back of the wagon.

The long day of roaming around, followed by the revelation that Bruce was still alive, ensured that Kingsley had put from his mind their concern that they had been followed. So when he saw movement ahead it took him a moment before he jerked back on the reins.

'Did you see that?' he asked.

'I saw a shadow move across the rock face,' Manville said.

The two men reached for their guns. A moment later an armed man stepped out from behind a rock ahead.

'Get down, Bruce,' Kingsley said, and then jumped down from the wagon. Manville leapt to the ground on his side of the wagon, and the two men scurried to the sides of the fissure. Kingsley stood against the rock face, and the undulating rock ensured he could no longer see the gunman.

Manville nodded to him across the pass, confirming he was also in a safe position. Then Bruce scrambled out of the back of the wagon with a gun in his hand.

He hurried towards Kingsley, although when he registered which side he'd chosen, he wavered. Then with a shrug, he joined him.

'What are we facing?' he asked.

'One gunman is ahead,' Kingsley said. 'Yesterday Manville saw several riders acting suspiciously. I didn't get a good look at this man, but if he's from that group there could be more of them.'

Bruce sighed. 'I haven't seen no trouble in seven years. Then I meet you and once again my life is in danger!'

'And just like the last time, I'll try to keep you safe.'

'This time I'll keep myself safe.' Bruce raised his

gun and patted it.

Kingsley smiled and edged towards the wagon until he saw the gunman, who had his hat lowered so it covered most of his face. The man jerked his gun towards Kingsley, who moved back, but not before his opponent blasted a gunshot that rattled off down the fissure.

'At least you've confirmed his intentions,' Manville called.

Manville then stepped forwards, but after taking three paces, two rapid shots tore out, making him hurry back.

'And we've confirmed he's pinned us all down,' Kingsley said.

'Perhaps if we acted in unison we'd have more luck.'

Kingsley nodded and raised four fingers as he began a countdown, but Bruce spoke up.

'That won't work,' he said.

'If you've got a better idea, speak up,' Kingsley said.

'I haven't got one and I don't care if you get holed, but Manville seems a decent man.' Bruce gestured at a high point ahead. 'Another gunman is on a ledge up there. You might be able to defeat the man on the ground, but I doubt you can deal with the one higher up.'

Kingsley looked up and he figured Bruce was right, as he saw several ledges that were large enough to hide a man.

He turned to Bruce. 'If we can't go forwards, we'll have to go back.'

'That won't help. This pass goes nowhere other than to the place where you found me.'

Kingsley shook his head. 'I don't believe you. You've explored this area for years, and you must have found another way out of here.'

Bruce sneered, but a shot blasted from ahead made him flinch. The shooter wasn't visible, but Kingsley reckoned he was closer than before.

Bruce must have come to the same conclusion, as he sighed and pointed back down the pass.

'All right, there is another way out. It's treacherous, but it doesn't look as if we have a choice.'

Kingsley gestured to Manville, and they all backed away. They were ten yards past the wagon when gunfire ripped out from high in the pass. Presumably the gunman on the ledge was firing. The man's position was so secure Kingsley couldn't even see him, so he beckoned for everyone to take flight.

They turned and ran. Slugs whined, but none of them came close, and after running for thirty seconds a bend in the pass took them out of the gunmen's line of fire. They still ran on for a while

102

before stopping and looking back at the quiet scene.

'They have my wagon and a defendable position, so they might not follow us,' Manville said.

Kingsley nodded. 'Unless they know about the other way out they'll probably wait for us to make another attempt to leave.'

'I doubt anybody knows about it,' Bruce said. He glanced at Manville. 'Although I gather your father often used it.'

'I knew you'd tell me some interesting things about him,' Manville said. 'I'd welcome hearing more.'

Bruce frowned, suggesting he'd spoken without thinking, and he now regretted doing so.

'Maybe later, when we're not running from trouble.'

With that they hurried on. Ten minutes later they approached the mound of boulders that blocked the pass, and Bruce signified he needed to catch his breath before they began their ascent.

They hadn't seen any sign of a pursuit, but Kingsley noted Manville's concerned expression.

'What's wrong?' he asked.

'I heard something,' Manville said.

'That's me struggling for breath,' Bruce gasped, but when Kingsley shot an irritated glance at him, he became silent and joined the others in listening.

For a minute all was quiet. Then Kingsley heard a man murmur an urgent demand from somewhere up the slope.

'Either they followed us in, or the other way out of the pass is no secret,' Kingsley said and then shrugged. 'Whatever the answer, we could be blocked in both directions.'

'Hopefully these men aren't trouble,' Manville said. 'But in case they are, do you know a third way out, Bruce?'

When Bruce shook his head they walked cautiously towards the nearest cover of a boulder at the base of the slope. They had taken only five paces when three gunmen stood up from behind covering rocks on the slope.

The gunmen fired, but they were some distance away and the shots peppered the dirt a dozen yards in front of them. Kingsley's group still took refuge at the side of the pass, and presently the gunmen dropped down from view.

'If we can reach the boulders we'll have cover,' Kingsley said. 'I reckon we could then defeat them.'

'We could, but can we even get there?' Manville said.

Kingsley agreed that the gunmen were in commanding positions, so he looked at Bruce for suggestions and the old prospector pointed back along the way they'd come.

'We're in trouble whichever way we go, but three men are ahead and two are behind us,' he said. 'So I say we turn back.'

Bruce was speaking sense, but Kingsley's growing irritation with the situation made him snarl and set off towards the slope. He walked sideways with his back to the rock face and his gun aimed at the boulders ahead, and after a few paces Manville joined him.

'When you see someone shoot, I'll run,' Kingsley said. 'When I reach the slope I'll cover you.'

Manville sighed, acknowledging this was a risky venture, but he nodded. They had taken twenty paces when Bruce hurried on to join them.

'This won't work,' he said. 'But at least I'll get to see you shot up.'

Kingsley started to snap back a retort, but he became silent when a gunman raised himself and fired, the shot clattering into the rock a foot above his head. Manville and Kingsley both aimed their guns at the man, but before they could return fire a second gunman fired at them.

Kingsley didn't see where the shot landed, but he thrust his head down and ran. As Manville blasted a barrage of covering fire, he figured he was thirty yards from safety.

He ran the first ten paces without problems. Then the gunmen hammered lead at him. The gunshots ploughed into the dirt a few yards ahead of him, promising him that if he carried on he'd be cut down.

Worse, Manville cried out. He glanced back and his colleague was fingering a bloodied cheek, and although the wound was only a nick he was no longer covering him.

Bruce wasn't firing either, so he slid to a halt and ran back towards them. His retreat encouraged Bruce to run away, and Manville loosed off a shot at the slope before fleeing with him.

Wild gunshots blasted behind them, but by the time the three men had returned to their earlier position the shooting had stopped. Kingsley checked out Manville's cheek confirming he'd been hit by a rock shard that had been blasted away by the gunfire.

He looked back. The gunmen had again dropped down, but he didn't reckon they'd fare any better with a second attempt to reach the boulders, so with a sorry shake of the head he beckoned for Bruce to lead the retreat.

'Going back is our only option,' Manville said. 'We can't reach the slope, never mind scale it.'

'I know, but it feels as if we're doing what the

gunmen want us to do,' Kingsley said. 'They fired a whole heap of lead and yet the only injury we suffered was your nick.'

Manville nodded. 'You reckon they just want to drive us away?'

Their debate made Bruce stop and turn to them.

'You could be right,' he said. 'They probably want gold, not us.'

Kingsley shrugged. 'You said you'd never had no luck back there.'

Bruce spread his arms to display his threadbare and grimed clothing.

'Do I look like a lucky man?'

'Sure. You're alive and that's more than—'

'That's enough!' Manville snapped. 'You two can argue when we're back in Prospect Town. For now we need to get past the gunmen, and I reckon we should test the theory that they want us to leave.'

With that Manville moved on, leaving Bruce and Kingsley to glare at each other before they followed him. When they'd rounded a bend and could see the wagon Manville rolled his shoulders and then broke into a run.

Kingsley and Bruce followed. With every step Kingsley expected gunfire, but they reached the tailboard without reprisals.

Manville shook a triumphant fist. Then they

clambered up into the wagon and crawled along to lie behind the seat.

'We need to do this quickly,' Kingsley said.

'Agreed,' Manville said. 'I'll take the reins, and you and Bruce watch out for trouble.'

When Kingsley nodded, he and Manville climbed into the seat. Kingsley couldn't see the gunmen, but he still trained his gun on the high ledge, while Bruce knelt down behind Manville and aimed at the side of the pass.

Manville got the wagon moving, and within a minute they drew level with the ledge and then passed it. Beyond that point the pass opened up and there was still no sign of anyone, so Kingsley leaned to the side to look back.

This time, two men were peering over the side of the ledge. When they saw they'd been noticed they ducked down, but not before Kingsley recognized them.

'They really do want us to leave,' Bruce said. 'So why did they block us the first time?'

'I reckon that was a warning,' Manville said. 'They were showing us, and anyone else who might be minded to come out here, the kind of trouble they'll face.'

Bruce sighed. 'I have no choice but to come back.'

'Thankfully I do, and as far as I'm concerned they

can do whatever they want out here.'

The entrance to the pass then came into view and Manville slowed down. A minute later they trundled into the valley where Manville headed to a position where they could watch the pass.

There was no sign of any other gunmen or of them being followed, so Manville turned to Kingsley for an opinion – but Kingsley didn't reply as he was trying to work out what his recent observation meant. When Manville nudged him, Kingsley gestured at the pass.

'Two gunmen were on the ledge, and I know who they are,' he said with a low tone to alert them to his revelation. 'They're Friedmann Jacobson and his associate Vandyke. Friedmann was one of the men I was running away from when I joined you in Hard Ridge.'

'Friedmann is after you?' Bruce spluttered.

Kingsley nodded. 'I thought I had the most to fear from Skelton, but it would seem I was wrong.'

'Seven years ago you ruined my chances of finding gold. Now you've done it again.'

'It's not the same, as I haven't shot you.' Kingsley smiled. 'Not that I need to, as this time Friedmann can do it when you come back.'

Bruce snarled, but then with a dismissive wave he turned his back on him. Manville glanced at him, and then at Kingsley. When both men showed no sign of prolonging their argument, he sighed and hurried the wagon back towards Prospect Town.

CHAPTER 11

It was late in the day when the three men approached Prospect Town. On the way back down the valley they had been quiet and had encountered no further problems. Ahead, the settlers had circled their wagons beyond the edge of town, but they were wandering around both outside and within the town as they became familiar with their new home.

'You've got some explaining to do now,' Kingsley said to Bruce.

'The only thing I'll do is make sure I never see you again,' Bruce said. 'You've ruined my life twice now, and I don't want to risk you doing it a third time.'

'And the only way you can make sure we don't cross paths again is for you to tell everyone the truth.'

Bruce opened his mouth to retort, but Manville

glared at him over his shoulder, warning him not to start an argument. Bruce sighed and folded his arms. Manville rode past the settlers to ensure that everyone saw him, and then moved into town. Thorndike and Norwell were standing outside the saloon, so he headed there and drew up.

'I didn't reckon you'd have the guts to show your face here again,' Thorndike called to Kingsley.

Kingsley ignored him and jumped down to the ground with Manville. Bruce showed his lack of interest in helping him by dallying, until with a reluctant grunt he shuffled out of the wagon and joined Manville.

'We came back so you could meet someone,' Manville said. He stepped aside and pointed. 'This is Bruce Russell.'

Thorndike looked Bruce up and down and shook his head.

'I don't know who that man is, but he sure looks alive to me,' he said.

'I am alive,' Bruce said, stepping forward. 'I've been brought back so Kingsley can make his peace with men like you. So know this: Kingsley is no friend of mine and I don't care how much of a bad time you give him, but you won't deny me the right to my name.'

Their exchange gathered the interest of several

men, including settlers and the original townsfolk. As these people gravitated towards them, Thorndike appraised Bruce and shrugged.

'Whoever you are, it doesn't change the fact that Kingsley killed someone and served time for it. We don't want his kind in Prospect Town.'

'He hasn't killed nobody! I'm the man they say he killed, except they got that wrong.'

'I don't believe—'

'Believe it,' Skelton said in a strident tone from within the saloon, making everyone turn to him as he pushed open the batwings and stood with a hand resting on each door. 'That's Bruce Russell, looking more alive than he did on the day I and Friedmann Jacobson thought Kingsley had killed him. It would seem we were wrong, and I owe both Bruce and Kingsley an apology.'

While Thorndike tipped back his hat in surprise and then showed his disgust with a curl of his lip, Kingsley stepped forwards to stand in front of the door.

'I welcome hearing that,' he said, 'and I welcome the chance to make a fresh start in your fine town.'

Skelton glanced at Kingsley before heading back into the saloon without comment. Thorndike walked towards Kingsley while rubbing his jaw, but then seemingly in acceptance of the fact that after

Skelton's declaration he could no longer cast doubt on him, he turned away and followed Skelton into the saloon.

Norwell joined him, and with the encounter over, the onlookers disbanded. Nobody met Kingsley's eye, although Manville nodded to several people and received brief acknowledgements in return.

'I've completed my obligation to you,' Bruce said while facing the saloon. 'I guess I should now renew my acquaintance with Skelton. Afterwards, I never want to see either of you two again.'

Without a further word he moved away, leaving Kingsley and Manville standing alone outside the saloon.

'I reckon that result was the best you could have hoped for,' Manville said after a while. 'Skelton's encouraged everyone to accept you, and Thorndike no longer has a way to turn everyone against you.'

'You're right, although Skelton didn't look pleased with this development,' Kingsley said. 'And it's doubtful whether Bruce will ever help you now.'

'When he's calmed down he might tell me something useful, provided you're not with me at the time.'

'If that's your way of telling me to keep my head down, I'm not doing that.' Kingsley then gestured at the saloon. 'Either way, I reckon my first taste of

114

liquor since leaving jail is long overdue.'

When Manville supported the suggestion with a grin, the two men headed inside.

CHAPTER 12

Only a handful of customers were in the saloon, and most of them were men Kingsley didn't recognize. Skelton and Bruce were sitting at a table beside the window, while Thorndike and Norwell were at one end of the bar. Kingsley headed to the opposite end, but as he didn't have any money he stood aside for Manville to buy them both whiskeys.

Thorndike watched them, but Kingsley ignored him as he leaned back against the bar; with his glass cradled against his chest he looked across the saloon room. Skelton and Bruce had their backs to him while they talked in low voices.

As it didn't look as if Manville would get a chance to question Bruce for a while, Kingsley started to turn away, but then Bruce removed a small bundle tied up in a rag from his pocket. He deposited it on the bar

and Skelton slipped it into his own pocket before set-
tling back in his chair.

Kingsley thought back, and recalled that Bruce
had pocketed a rock before they'd left his shelter.
Kingsley watched them, but as they then only talked
he turned around.

'Have you figured out yet why Friedmann ran us
out of the pass?' Manville said, and then sipped his
whiskey. 'He surely can't have followed you there and
then decided to stay to look for gold.'

Kingsley raised the glass to his lips and then
lowered it without drinking.

'I had the same thought as you. Then again,
Friedmann's behaviour in Hard Ridge was odd. He
told me Skelton was in town and he planned to kill
me.' Kingsley rubbed his chin. 'Then, when I
escaped, his attempt to recapture me was surprisingly
inept.'

'Are you saying he wanted you to escape so he
could follow you to a place where he could dig for
gold?'

'Maybe, but the problem is I had no intention of
looking for gold, and I have no idea where to find it.'
Kingsley glanced over his shoulder at Bruce. 'But I'm
now wondering if Bruce knows where to look after
all, and Friedmann was really searching for him.'

Manville nodded. 'Bruce has been evasive, as if he

has something to hide.'

'I agree. So when he's finished with Skelton I reckon you should get some proper answers from him.'

Manville nodded, as behind them Skelton muttered an oath. Both men turned to find that Skelton was scraping back his chair.

Skelton leapt to his feet and glared at Bruce, his behaviour making the other customers stare at them. He raised a fist, and he looked as if he was about to hit Bruce or at least say something that would reveal the reason for his anger, but then he glanced around and winced as he appeared to register that he had an audience.

With a shake of the head he lowered his fist and stormed off to the door. At the bar, Thorndike and Norwell put down their glasses and without even discussing how they should react, walked across the saloon room and followed him out.

Bruce stayed sitting, and after a few moments the other customers returned to their previous business – but with a nod to each other, Kingsley and Manville headed to Bruce's table. They sat on either side of Bruce, who looked at them with a resigned expression, by which he appeared to accept he couldn't make light of what had just happened.

'I assume you now regret renewing your acquaintance with Skelton,' Manville said with a smile.

'I never wanted to come here,' Bruce muttered. 'When you forced me to make the journey I had no choice but to talk with him.'

'From what I've understood about what happened seven years ago, Skelton has no reason to still be angry with you.'

'Leave me alone. I don't have to explain nothing.'

Manville glanced at Kingsley, presumably to direct him to leave in the hope that Bruce would be more forthcoming, but Kingsley shook his head and leaned towards Bruce.

'You don't,' he said. 'But I reckon you don't want to explain because that wasn't the first time you've met Skelton in the last seven years. He knew you were alive, while *you* know that Friedmann came looking for you, not me, and Skelton wasn't pleased to hear about it.'

Bruce stood up to leave, but then he rocked from foot to foot and with a resigned shrug sat back down again. He glanced around, and although none of the customers were near enough to hear him, he still spoke quietly.

'Sure,' he said.

'You gave Skelton something you pocketed before we left your shelter. To me it looked like a small rock, but I reckon that might have been gold.'

Bruce lowered his head. 'It was.'

'I also reckon you've done that before.' Kingsley waited for a response, but Bruce didn't reply. 'So why are you giving Skelton your gold?'

Bruce rubbed his brow. Then with a frown he raised his head and looked at the two men in turn.

'Everyone here knows the story of how Skelton built Prospect Town up from nothing, but nobody ever asks how he paid for it.'

Manville leaned back in his chair and groaned, while Kingsley nodded.

'Skelton isn't a visionary businessman,' Kingsley said. 'He's just using your gold.'

'He has a vision,' Bruce said with a shrug. 'It's just not the one he claims to have. If this town prospers, he'll become everything he wants to be. If it doesn't, he'll have lost nothing.'

'What do you gain out of this arrangement?'

Bruce glanced at Manville before turning his chair to face Kingsley. When he spoke his voice was more assured than before, suggesting that now he'd revealed his secret he felt more confident.

'When I returned to Hard Ridge seven years ago I met Skelton. He convinced me that he hadn't intended to cause me harm, and I convinced him that I knew the area where Creighton Frost had found gold, even if I didn't know the exact spot. He promised that when he could afford it he'd finance

120

me on another search.'

'And this time you were successful?'

'In the end I was. It took me four years, but when I started finding gold I couldn't stop. For a while everything was fine, but Friedmann worked out what we were doing. Skelton had been grateful for what he'd done for him and had given him money, but he didn't tell him about me. Friedmann felt cheated and searched for me. Once he even explored the pass, but I hid and he moved on.'

Kingsley nodded. 'So I was right. Friedmann figured my release from jail was an opportunity to find you.'

Bruce shrugged. 'Whether he hoped you'd find me, or he just wanted to wind you up to go after Skelton, I don't know. The result is the same, as Friedmann now controls the pass where I've been finding the gold.'

'What will Skelton do about it?'

'He sounded annoyed enough to remove him by force, but if he does nothing I'll drive him away myself.' Bruce shook a fist. 'Seven years ago Friedmann left me to die. I'll not accept that man cheating me again.'

'Friedmann thought you were dead.'

'Would you have mistaken a live man for a dead one?' Bruce looked at Kingsley and when Kingsley

121

shrugged, he frowned. 'I guess I'll probably never know for sure, but I've always reckoned that he knew what he was doing, so he's as much to blame as you are.'

'If he did that, he's more to blame. He left you deliberately, while I only shot you accidentally.'

'That was no accident.' Bruce stood up and started to walk away.

'It was,' Kingsley called after him. 'I thought you'd thrown a branch at me, but I wasn't to know you threw it at Skelton.'

Bruce took another pace towards the door, but then stopped and turned back. He kicked at the floor as if he was embarrassed about what he was about to say.

'As I've told you, I struggle to remember most of what happened that night, but I'll admit one thing: after you shot Skelton I panicked and threw a branch at you. Either way, it was only wood, and you retaliated with lead.'

Bruce cast him a sneering glance and then resumed his walk to the door. This time Kingsley was still reeling from Bruce's revelation, and he didn't try to stop him.

'I can't recall enough about the incident to know why that's shocked you,' Manville said when Bruce had left the saloon.

'I always thought that it was *me* whom Bruce attacked,' Kingsley said. 'I fought back only to defend myself, but at the trial Friedmann said the branch had been aimed at Skelton. As I'd made a mistake, I accepted my punishment.'

Manville winced. 'So Friedmann lied, and maybe if he'd told the truth you'd have been deemed to have acted in self-defence.'

'It's possible, and as I was wrong about him being more reasonable than Skelton was, he probably lied about reckoning Bruce was dead, too, and he must have saved Skelton only because he had money.' Kingsley glanced outside at the darkening sky. 'It's too late to go back to the pass today, but tomorrow, whether or not Skelton and Bruce go after Friedmann, I'm going there to get some answers.'

Manville smiled. 'In that case I'm coming with you, and we'll find out what's going on.'

Kingsley shook his head. 'I came up against Friedmann's gunmen in Hard Ridge. They'll be tough to take on, and this argument has got nothing to do with you.'

'I don't frighten easily, and besides, Friedmann and Skelton and Bruce are fighting over the place where my father found gold. I reckon that somehow the answer to what happened to him is tied up in all this.'

'I can't see how, but I guess you might still learn more about . . .' Kingsley trailed off and looked upwards, as Manville's theory made him consider something he hadn't thought about before.

'What have you just figured out?' Manville asked.

Kingsley rubbed his jaw as he worked through the ramifications of his worrying new idea. He was unwilling to voice it unless he was sure, but no matter how he looked at it, his theory felt as if it was the only possible explanation for Bruce's evasive behaviour.

He sighed, and leaned towards Manville.

'Bruce has answered only some of our questions, and even then I doubt he's been completely truthful. Even just now when he was being more open, he ignored my question about what he gains from giving the gold to Skelton.'

Manville rubbed his jaw while he pondered, and then nodded.

'Bruce doesn't look prosperous while Skelton sure does, but Bruce said that Skelton financed him, so maybe he's repaying his debt.'

'Maybe he is, but not all debts are financial. What if the debt Bruce owes to Skelton is of a different kind?'

Manville narrowed his eyes. 'Connected to what happened seven years ago?'

'In a way it is.' Kingsley frowned and lowered his

124

voice. 'Bruce convinced Skelton he knew where your father found the nugget. What if his story led to Skelton figuring out a secret about Bruce?'

Manville gulped and his mouth dropped open as he came to the same shocking conclusion that had occurred to Kingsley.

'Are you saying that Bruce was my father's partner?'

Kingsley nodded. 'I am, and that means he's the man who killed him.'

CHAPTER 13

'As we expected, Skelton's leaving early,' Manville said the following morning. Kingsley joined him in standing beside his wagon, and they watched the riders head out of town. Skelton was leading a group of six men who included Thorndike and Norwell from the settlers, with the rest coming from the original townsfolk.

'Bruce is not amongst them, so what do you want to do?' Kingsley said.

'I figure he'll get involved on his own, probably by sneaking into the pass using his secret way. So we'll wait until he makes his move.'

Kingsley glanced into town, and he wasn't surprised that Bruce was already heading to the stable. The sight made Manville mutter under his breath and make his way towards town. The previous night they hadn't discussed their theory about Bruce, but Manville's stern-set jaw suggested he'd done plenty of thinking, and his opinion hadn't changed. Fearing that Manville might do something he'd regret, Kingsley hurried past him so he could intercept Bruce first.

'Are you planning to get a horse and follow Skelton?' he called.

Bruce stopped outside the stable. 'I don't have to answer any more of your questions.'

'You don't, but I reckon we can all agree that Friedmann has questions to answer and he's holed up in the pass. If we're together, we'll have a better chance of getting what we want.'

'We will, but that doesn't mean we should ride together.'

Kingsley set his hands on his hips as he struggled to think of a way to talk him round, but Manville then joined them.

'My father would have wanted us to sort this out together,' he said. 'After all, he had more of a right to dictate what goes on there than anyone else does.'

Bruce glanced away and to Kingsley's surprise he gave a brief nod.

'I assume we can go back there on your wagon,' he said.

When Manville nodded, Bruce moved on.

Kingsley and Manville dallied to look at each other, acknowledging that when Manville had mentioned his father, Bruce had acquiesced, adding weight to the possibility he had a guilty conscience.

By the time they left town Skelton's group was no longer visible, but they didn't try to catch up with them. They figured that would give Skelton time to confront Friedmann and to take the greater risks.

When they approached the pass Bruce directed Manville to go into the gulch. Then they headed past their campsite from seven years ago to a place where the side of the gulch was almost sheer, confirming Bruce's contention that the secret way into the pass was treacherous.

Bruce pointed at an outcrop of rock that was higher than the surrounding land. At first Kingsley couldn't see the route, and when he located a path that involved moving upwards along narrow and sloping ledges, he gave a loud whistle and tipped back his hat.

'You did promise there was no easy way in,' he said.

'Which means it should give us the element of surprise, provided we keep our footing,' Bruce said.

Manville took the wagon to the base of the outcrop. Bruce alighted first and set off on the climb.

The first fifty feet were difficult to ascend. Bruce

led them up a route where they had to hold on to bumps in the rock and drag themselves higher while pressing their bodies to the rock face. Once they reached the first ledge the going became easier and they were able to walk along ledges that gradually took them higher.

'I'd guess the difficult start is what's stopped people from noticing this path before,' Manville said when they were halfway to the summit.

Bruce nodded. 'When I first found it I was coming down and I didn't reach the tricky section until the end. After that, it was easier to go down instead of climbing back up.'

After this exchange and as they were now high off the ground, they reverted to silence and concentrated on the ascent. The challenge appeared to rejuvenate the old prospector, as he led the way at such a fast pace he had to stop several times for the others to catch up with him.

It took them thirty minutes to reach a plateau that spread out to either side of them and ahead for several miles. When Kingsley and Manville had given each other a slap on the back in celebration, they all sat back against the tip of the massive rock formation they'd seen from ground level and took deep breaths as they recovered from the ascent.

When he'd got his breath back, Kingsley glanced

down. The sheer drop to the ground below made him giddy and he jerked his head back. He figured that going down would be more of an ordeal than going up had been, as he would then see the long drop to the ground more often. He resolved he'd come back this way only if he had no choice.

Manville also looked down and gave a startled expression that confirmed he'd had the same thought.

They turned away. Bruce led them across the plateau towards the gash in the rock where they'd first come across him. When they could see down to ground level, it was clear that during their previous visit they had seen only a small section of the area, as the tangle of boulders stretched for some distance beyond Bruce's shelter.

'Where's the exact place where my father found the nugget?' Manville said.

'I keep telling you that I don't know,' Bruce said with a weary air. 'I just know the general area, and for the last few years I explored until I had some success.'

'But it's near to the shelter that you made your base?'

Bruce shrugged. 'I believe that Creighton rested there, so I reckoned it was good enough for me, too.'

Bruce beckoned for them to be quiet, after which

they moved closer to the gash with their heads down. When they could see the whole area they lowered themselves to their knees.

'It'd seem that Friedmann hasn't started looking for gold yet,' Kingsley said when five minutes had passed without them seeing anyone below.

'Perhaps Skelton is keeping him busy at the other end of the pass,' Manville said. 'So we could play the trick on him that he carried out with us and trap him from both sides.'

Kingsley nodded, but Bruce shook his head.

'If you want to do that, you're welcome to try,' he said. 'I'll let Skelton deal with Friedmann while I regain control of my domain.'

Kingsley was about to disagree, but Manville accepted his suggestion with a smile.

'That makes sense,' he said. 'If we have the high ground, we can wait for Friedmann to come to us. Then we can fight him off with ease.'

Bruce shrugged, as if Manville's agreement wasn't important to him. Then he pointed out a path through the mass of boulders that would bring them out beside his shelter. The route was convoluted, leaving them dependent on Bruce to direct them, but the prospector looked confident, and ten minutes later they emerged into a clear area. The edge of the slope was fifty yards ahead, while the box containing the rocks was still sitting proud on a boulder where Bruce had left it.

They moved on, and were level with the shelter when shouting could be heard ahead. Kingsley judged it was coming from the bottom of the slope. With the commotion suggesting they'd arrived at a crucial time, they moved on cautiously. Raised voices sounded again, and this time Kingsley heard Skelton issuing an order.

'It sounds as if Skelton has managed to get here quickly,' Kingsley said.

'So either he's defeated Friedmann, or Friedmann will be retreating up here,' Manville said.

With that, he and Manville speeded up, although Bruce stayed back. They hurried to the edge of the slope, but when they peered down, Kingsley couldn't see anyone.

'Skelton must have gone to ground down there somewhere,' he said.

When Manville shrugged, he turned to ask Bruce for his opinion, but Bruce had turned his back on them and had raised his hands. Kingsley looked past him and saw that the four men who had accosted him in Hard Ridge had already reached the summit.

These men were now standing in front of the shelter with their guns trained on them. With a wince Kingsley raised his hands, and when Manville saw what he was doing he turned around and groaned, then followed his lead. Only then did another man emerge from the shelter to face them. His arrival made Bruce take a step backwards, while Kingsley joined Manville in groaning.

'I knew you'd come back here,' Friedmann Jacobson said with a smile. 'Unfortunately, that means you won't ever get to leave.'

CHAPTER 14

'So you got me here in the end,' Kingsley said, when Vandyke and Rex had disarmed them and made them drop on their knees in front of the shelter. 'Was that your plan all along?'

'I had intended to rile you up so you'd go to Prospect Town to deal with your problems,' Friedmann said. 'As it turned out, you didn't need no provocation to solve everything for me.'

'So you wanted to know where Bruce was finding the gold to finance Skelton's activities?'

Friedmann walked back and forth in front of them, seemingly making him wait for an answer, although Kingsley noted that he glanced over the edge of the slope, suggesting he knew Skelton was close.

'Seven years ago we all agreed to be partners, but

when Skelton reckoned Bruce could lead him to gold after all, he ignored that agreement.'

'You have a right to be aggrieved, but that was a long time ago. All our lives are different now, and not all of us have prospered.'

'You got what you deserved,' Friedmann snarled.

'Maybe I did, but I've made my peace with Skelton and Bruce. Perhaps it's time you did the same instead of trying to get rich at the end of a gun.'

Friedmann glanced at Bruce and smiled. 'Bruce's sneer when you made that claim suggests he hasn't forgiven you, but no matter. He'll now give me what I want.'

Friedmann moved on to stand over Bruce, who shook his head.

'You haven't changed,' he said. 'Seven years ago you thought I could just walk around picking up gold nuggets off the ground, and you're no more informed now. It takes months, sometimes years, to find anything. I can't just show you gold straight-away.'

'I know that, but you've misunderstood my purpose.' Friedmann smiled. 'I don't want to join you in scrabbling around in the dirt. I only wanted to prove what you and Skelton have been doing here.'

Friedmann withdrew a small bag from his pocket and waved it above his head, making the contents clunk against each other.

'You found my stash of finds,' Bruce murmured unhappily.

'I sure have, and as you've walked back into my domain I now want my share of everything you've found, and will find.'

Bruce frowned. 'And if you don't get it, you'll kill me?'

'If I have to, but I don't reckon it'll come to that. Skelton won't want his reputation ruined by the proof that he's not the accomplished businessman he claims to be, and I reckon you have your secrets.'

Bruce flinched and shot a sideways glance at Manville, his behaviour possibly confirming Friedmann's assumption as well as the nature of that secret. In response, Manville changed his stance so he was kneeling with one knee raised.

'I agree to your terms, but Skelton won't,' Bruce said.

Friedmann pocketed the bag and moved to the edge of the slope. He frowned and directed Larry and Halford to join him.

'We'll see what he says. He'll be with us presently.' Friedmann cleared his throat and then bellowed down the slope. 'Skelton, Bruce did what I wanted him to do when I let him leave. He's riled you up so much you came out here. Even better, he and the others have returned, so now I have hostages.'

Muttered cries of alarm sounded, making Friedmann chuckle. A minute passed and then Skelton called out.

'What do you want?' he shouted.

'Talk terms or I'll kill them and destroy everything you're trying to do here.'

'That's plenty for me to think about.'

'You have five minutes to do that thinking. Then I start throwing bodies down to you.'

Friedmann moved away from the edge of the slope and began pacing, leaving Larry and Halford watching Skelton, and Vandyke and Rex guarding the hostages.

'So you have a secret, Bruce,' Manville whispered from the corner of his mouth. 'And you're so desperate to keep it you gave up the gold without a word of complaint.'

'I'm trying to save our lives,' Bruce said.

'We're grateful for that, but what kind of secret could you have when you were reluctant to talk to me about my father?'

'I didn't speak about Creighton because I have nothing to tell you,' Bruce said, raising his voice to a level that made Friedmann stop pacing and turn to them.

'And you say that while we're in the place where

my father found the nugget and you're being forced to reveal its location.' Manville raised a hand when Bruce started to reply. 'Don't say that you've only recently figured out where to look.'

Manville glared at Bruce, but their discussion made Friedmann move closer while pointing at them. Both men ignored him as they faced each other.

'Then I won't say that,' Bruce said, his voice small.

'I've already worked out the truth about my father's murder in Pine Springs,' Manville said, his voice now strained. 'Just admit you killed him.'

Vandyke looked at Friedmann for direction, and as Manville and Bruce continued to face each other, Friedmann spoke up.

'That's enough,' he said. 'Separate them.'

Vandyke and Rex stepped forwards and moved to take hold of one man apiece, but before they could lay hands on either of them Bruce nodded.

'I'm sorry,' he said. 'I did it. I killed him.'

Manville roared with anger and leapt forwards with his hands rising to grab Bruce's throat. At the last moment Bruce jerked backwards evading Manville's clutches, but Manville still bundled him over on to his back.

Vandyke and Rex moved to drag them apart, while Friedmann smirked as he watched the altercation.

With this skirmish holding everyone's attention Kingsley rolled back on to his haunches and stood up.

Their confiscated guns had been thrown towards Bruce's box. They were too far away to reach, so when nobody reacted to his movement Kingsley turned and with his head down, ran towards the shelter.

He pounded along for half the distance before Vandyke shouted a warning. He still ran on, but when he swung around the side of the shelter he came to a sudden halt. Another boulder was ahead and blocking his way.

As Friedmann muttered an order to his men, Kingsley decided his only option was to climb on to the top of the shelter. The rock was smooth, but it was also rounded, so he raised his right foot and hoisted himself up.

As he felt secure, he placed his left foot higher up the side, but rapid footfalls sounded behind him and when he glanced down Friedmann was running towards him.

Friedmann stopped below Kingsley and grabbed his lower leg. He tugged, dragging him back down, but Kingsley's grip of the side must have been stronger than he thought as Friedmann failed to dislodge him.

Emboldened, he twisted round, and with his side braced against the rock, he kicked out. His boot slammed into Friedmann's chest, tipping him over, so Kingsley twisted back to the boulder and clambered up it.

Scrambling sounded as Friedmann gained his feet, and his hand closed around Kingsley's ankle but his grip was weak. Kingsley squirmed until he freed himself, and then kept climbing until he was lying on the flat rock above the shelter.

He glanced over his shoulder. Friedmann was no longer visible so he moved across the rock to the front.

Larry and Halford were looking down the slope and the fighting prisoners had been separated, but Vandyke and Rex were facing him. Kingsley ducked down, the action saving him when both men fired at him. Dust flew as the bullets nicked the edge of the rock, so he dropped down on to his belly. Another burst of gunfire followed, but he didn't reckon those shots had been aimed at him.

He raised his head and saw that Larry and Halford were blasting lead down the slope. Skelton must be making a decisive move as Larry cried out and toppled backwards with his chest blooded.

When Halford dropped down to get out of Skelton's line of sight, Friedmann shouted an order to Vandyke and Rex. These men moved away to help Halford, and as Bruce and Manville were no longer being guarded they put aside their argument and set off after them.

They were five paces away from the gunmen when Vandyke stopped and turned his gun on Bruce, making both men skid to a halt. Then gunfire again rattled from Skelton's group, and as the sounds were closer than the previous shots had been, Rex carried on and joined Halford to exchange fire.

Kingsley stood up and put his thoughts to how he could help his colleagues, but then grit scraped behind him. He swirled round while lowering his head, and faced the advancing Friedmann, who had reached the top of the shelter quietly. His quick action saved him from a round-armed swipe that whistled over his shoulders. Friedmann settled his stance and shot an angry glare at him.

'It's all going wrong for you, Friedmann,' Kingsley said. 'Skelton will be here shortly and he's sure to overcome you.'

'I still have three hostages,' Friedmann said. He smirked with confidence. 'He won't care about what happens to you, but he won't risk any harm coming to Bruce.'

'You could be right, but the thing is: he knows you won't harm Bruce.'

141

Friedmann frowned, confirming that Kingsley's taunt was valid, but then gunfire thundered behind him. Kingsley turned to find that Rex was falling over, having been shot by Skelton's group.

Another volley of shots ripped out and lead scythed into Halford's stomach, making him drop to his knees.

Vandyke turned to go to his aid, so Bruce took advantage of the distraction. He broke into a run, and even when Vandyke turned back and aimed his gun at his chest he continued running.

'Don't shoot him!' Friedmann called.

A moment later Bruce reached Vandyke, who fired, tearing a slug into Bruce's chest from close quarters. Bruce stumbled on and barged into his opponent, knocking him back a pace.

Vandyke righted himself, but Bruce was dropping down and with a clawed hand he grabbed Vandyke's jacket and made him hunch over. Manville then pounded towards them, and from the corner of his eye, Kingsley saw Friedmann turn his gun on him.

Kingsley swirled round to confront Friedmann and lunged forwards. He grabbed Friedmann's gun arm and stopped it moving before thrusting the arm to the side.

Friedmann retaliated with a punch to Kingsley's stomach that made him fold over. Then he delivered an uppercut to Kingsley's chin that made him release his opponent's arm and stumble away.

Kingsley stopped himself after two paces, but his back foot landed on the curved end of the boulder and he slipped down. As he wheeled his arms trying to regain his balance, behind him a gunshot thundered and Vandyke cried out in pain.

A rapid burst of gunfire followed, but Kingsley couldn't tell who was firing as his attempt to stay upright failed and he tumbled backwards. He tipped all the way over and landed on his chest with a bone-jarring thud.

He lay winded, feeling like a bug that had been squashed beneath a boot. Rattling was sounding nearby, but as his senses were disorientated it took him a few moments to work out that gunshots were still being traded.

He slapped his hands to the ground and raised himself. His arms shook, but he figured that as he could move he hadn't been seriously hurt, and he forced himself to get up.

When he was on his feet he stood stooped over. Manville hurried towards him with an arm held out to help him, but Kingsley raised a hand to show he was fine and looked past him.

Bruce was lying where he'd been shot, while Vandyke lay beside him on his back with his chest blooded, presumably having been hit by one of Skelton's men. Further away Friedmann's other gunmen were on the ground and lying still.

Skelton was shouting something from out of his view on the slope, so Kingsley looked for Friedmann on the top of the shelter, but couldn't see him.

'When he saw that the situation was lost he went to ground,' Manville said, joining him in looking up.

'Which means he has to be close by,' Kingsley said.

He set off towards the side of the shelter. He stumbled on his first step, but with a roll of the shoulders he settled his stance and started walking again. This time he moved more effectively, and reached a position where he could see round the side of the shelter. Friedmann wasn't climbing down so he shrugged at Manville, who moved away from him to look round the other side of the shelter.

Manville flinched aside and a moment later a gunshot blasted from out of Kingsley's view. Kingsley hurried over to join Manville, who pointed.

'Friedmann is about to hightail it out of here, so he must know about Bruce's secret way.'

Kingsley edged forwards and confirmed that Manville had been right. Friedmann was backing away as he sought to slip into the jumble of boulders behind the shelter.

When Friedmann saw Kingsley he tipped his hat in

a mocking salute and then turned on his heels and ran. Kingsley sighed and held out a hand to Manville.

'Give me your gun,' he said. 'I'll deal with Friedmann while you look after Bruce and make sure those gunmen don't fight back.'

The first request made Manville sneer, but he handed over the gun and patted Kingsley's back before hurrying towards the sprawled bodies of the gunmen.

Kingsley watched Manville until he'd collected another gun and was holding it on the nearest gunman while cautiously checking whether he was still alive. Manville didn't check on Bruce, but he put that matter from his mind and hurried after Friedmann.

CHAPTER 15

Kingsley ran into the warren of boulders after his quarry, building up speed as he shook off the effects of his fall. He reckoned Friedmann was taking the route they had used on their way to the shelter, but within moments Friedmann disappeared from view.

Kingsley tried to recall the rest of the route, without success, and when a boulder blocked his path he had to double back.

At one stage he glimpsed Friedmann, and he was several dozen yards ahead of him. Then the terrain took him out of sight and he again became lost.

Kingsley's frustration was making him mutter oaths under his breath when he rounded a boulder and open ground was ahead.

He ducked down and looked for Friedmann, and saw him fleeing across the plateau several hundred yards away. He was heading towards the massive rock formation that marked the position of Bruce's secret way out of the pass, although he was veering from side to side suggesting that he might only have seen them coming from that direction, and didn't know its exact location.

Kingsley moved on cautiously, and when he could see down into the gash, Skelton and his men had reached the summit. The shot gunmen and Bruce were lying on the ground, but none of Skelton's men appeared to have been injured.

Skelton and Manville were exchanging views with much waving of arms. They both glanced at Bruce's body, suggesting the nature of the argument, but Kingsley judged that the debate was measured and wouldn't erupt into violence.

Then he followed Friedmann, who had reached the large rock. He was around fifty paces away from the place where they had climbed up, and after a glance downwards and at Kingsley, he moved on.

When he was close to the place where they'd rested up after their ascent, Friedmann looked down again. Then he clambered over the edge of the plateau and disappeared from view.

Kingsley winced and speeded up, reaching the rock in another minute. He moved on with his head down until he stood a few feet away from the spot where Friedmann had started his descent.

With his gun thrust out he rocked forwards to peer down. The nearest ledge was clear, and when he looked further down he still couldn't see Friedmann.

He didn't want to pursue his quarry down the sheer rock face, but if Friedmann reached the bottom he could escape on Manville's wagon. He moved forwards and to the side, hoping to find an angle where he could see and then shoot at him.

A hand shot up over the edge and grabbed his right ankle. The shock made Kingsley stumble backwards and fall over on to his back. Friedmann then dragged his foot forwards, making his lower leg slide over the edge. With a frantic movement Kingsley dug in his left heel and anchored himself.

Friedmann tugged once more, but when that failed to move Kingsley he raised himself into full view and leapt forwards: he landed on Kingsley's chest, pinning his arms to the ground and knocking the air out of his lungs.

With Kingsley floundering, Friedmann dragged him up to a crouched position and bundled him along towards the edge. Kingsley was still winded, but when he could see the drop down to the ground he squirmed as he sought to regain his strength.

He freed his left arm from Friedmann's clutches and tried to leap aside, but Friedmann still had a firm grip of his right arm and he continued to push.

Kingsley's right boot landed on the edge of the plateau before slipping down, pitching him forwards. Friedmann released his arm and stepped back, leaving Kingsley teetering.

With a desperate move he twisted, but his left foot slipped downwards. He fell, but only for a moment, and he landed with his upper body still on level ground and his legs dangling and pressed against the rock face.

He thrust both hands out to the side and clutched the rock. When he was sure he wouldn't slip down further he looked up to find that Friedmann was standing in front of him with his gun trained on him.

'You have a choice,' Friedmann said. 'Get shot and fall, or just fall.'

Kingsley strained his arms as he tried to manoeuvre his body back on to level ground, but Friedmann shook his head, making him desist.

'Everyone knows what kind of man you are now, Friedmann,' Kingsley said. 'You won't escape justice again.'

'I reckon I will. Vandyke shot Bruce in self-defence, just like you did seven years ago, and the other men got shot up by Skelton's men. I did nothing wrong back there, and there are no witnesses to what's about to happen here.'

'Your lies will catch you out in the end.'

Friedmann laughed. 'That threat fails to chill my blood. Now decide how you want this to end.'

Friedmann raised his gun slightly for emphasis, so Kingsley met Friedmann's eye.

'You destroyed my life, but you won't end it.'

Kingsley let his arms go slack. As he was no longer straining to stop himself slipping backwards, his lower body slid down. Then he fell. As the rock face went blurring by, he heard Friedmann murmur in surprise – but Kingsley fell for only a moment before his feet crunched down on to a ledge.

He had figured that as Friedmann had reached up and grabbed his ankle, one of the ledges he'd used when he'd ascended the outcrop had to be below. The ledge was only two feet wide, but with his theory turning out to be valid, he sighed with relief and drew his gun.

He aimed at a spot directly above him, as he figured Friedmann would check on his fate quickly.

Sure enough, a few seconds later Friedmann's head appeared as he looked down. He was standing a few feet away from where Kingsley had expected him to appear, so by the time he had snapped his gun round to aim at him, Friedmann was darting back.

'You got lucky, but you're just postponing the inevitable,' Friedmann called.

'That makes two of us,' Kingsley said. 'That gunfire will bring a whole heap of gunmen here to deal with you.'

In truth Kingsley doubted that Skelton would send anyone to help him, but he hoped Manville might come. He looked along the ledge.

The route to the summit was to his right. As he figured that Friedmann would expect him to try to reach the top, he stepped sideways to his left for five paces.

He levelled his gun at the spot where he would have emerged if he'd climbed up. A moment later Friedmann came into view with his gun aimed down, but he'd moved in the same direction that Kingsley had.

Friedmann grinned at his success in second-guessing Kingsley, and blasted two quick shots before Kingsley could take aim at him. The slugs sliced into the ledge a foot to his side, and by the time Kingsley returned fire, Friedmann had retreated.

With a snarl of anger Kingsley abandoned trying to work out what Friedmann would do next, and scrambled along the ledge. He worked his way higher while keeping his body as close to the rock face as he could.

As he was concentrating on where he placed his feet, he couldn't watch out for what was happening

151

above. With every pace he expected Friedmann to look down and start shooting, but he closed on the summit without Friedmann acting.

When he reached a point where his head was a few feet below the edge, he stopped. He listened, but heard no sounds other than the wind whipping by.

For Friedmann not to have taken another shot at him, Kingsley supposed he must have been feeling vulnerable. In the hope that help was coming, he lowered his head and hurried up the last few paces until he was standing crouched over below the plateau.

Then he slapped his left hand on the edge and used it to boost his vault up to the summit. The moment he'd righted himself he glanced around while swinging his gun to either side until he saw a running figure.

The man was a hundred yards away, and Kingsley had taken aim at him when he registered that it was Manville and that he was heading towards him.

Manville's arrival had presumably made Friedmann go to ground, so Kingsley waved to his colleague and then looked to either side. He didn't see his opponent, but when Manville gestured at the large rock he noted that it provided plenty of places where Friedmann could have holed up.

While looking for potential hiding places he

moved towards the outcrop. His gaze rested on a series of jagged protrusions that would have allowed Friedmann to climb up.

He aimed at the top of the rock and stopped twenty yards away. Manville hurried closer, but then with a grunt of alarm he skidded to a halt.

Kingsley couldn't see what had worried him, but a gunshot blasted. Friedmann had fired, but he still couldn't see where he had holed up, and when Manville went down on one knee, he accepted that he didn't know either.

Kingsley broke into a run and reached the base of the rock as Manville shouted a warning. Then in a blur of motion Friedmann jumped down from above.

Manville's warning gave Kingsley enough time to jerk aside, but Friedmann still caught him a glancing blow to the shoulder.

Kingsley stumbled to the side. He thrust out a leg, and when that failed to stop him, he went tumbling down on to his hands and knees.

The jarring blow knocked his gun from his grasp and it skittered away across the hard rock. When it stopped a dozen yards away he decided not to go after it.

Instead, he leapt to his feet while twisting round, finding that Friedmann had landed on his feet and was facing him. Friedmann snapped up his arm and aimed his gun at Kingsley's chest.

In desperation Kingsley ran towards him. Then a gunshot ripped out from behind him, making Friedmann arch his back.

Kingsley had just registered that Manville had shot Friedmann when he reached his target. On the run he slammed a round-armed blow into Friedmann's jaw that sent him teetering backwards with a hand clutched to his wounded side.

Before Friedmann could recover, Kingsley delivered an uppercut to his chin that snapped his head back, then drew back his fist for a pile-driver of a punch that would ground him. Then he found that he didn't need to hit his adversary again.

Friedmann had moved to the edge of the plateau, his position the same as the one Kingsley had found himself in a short while earlier.

As Friedmann fought for balance he raised a hand from his chest and wheeled his arms. But he still rocked backwards, and he met Kingsley's eyes with an imploring look.

Kingsley spread his hands, showing that he wouldn't help him. Then Friedmann toppled over backwards and disappeared from view.

Kingsley hurried away to collect his gun, and then waited for Manville to join him. When the two men looked over the edge they saw that Friedmann hadn't had the luck that had saved Kingsley: he was lying at the bottom of the outcrop with dust still rising up around his body.

'We had no choice,' Manville said. 'He wouldn't have hesitated to kill any one of us.'

'I know that,' Kingsley said. 'Sometimes we have to stop people from harming others in any way we can, but that doesn't make us bad men.'

Manville patted Kingsley's shoulder. 'It doesn't.'

CHAPTER 16

'How is Bruce?' Kingsley called to Skelton when he and Manville emerged from the tangled heap of boulders to stand beside the shelter.

'He's dead, as are Friedmann's hired guns,' Skelton said.

He gestured at the line of bodies and then at Thorndike and the rest of his men, drawing their attention to the fact that everyone on his side was unharmed. He raised an eyebrow requesting information on Friedmann's fate.

'I knocked Friedmann off the outcrop and he won't have survived the fall.'

'And he had one of my bullets in him,' Manville said.

Skelton nodded and smiled at both men, displaying

none of his usual antipathy now that the crisis was over.

'There's no need for you two to worry,' he said. 'This time there'll be no repercussions and it'll be clear to everyone that Friedmann is the only one to blame for this situation.'

Kingsley couldn't help but glance at Thorndike. For once Thorndike returned his gaze without his customary sneer. That was good enough for Kingsley, and he moved on to stand beside Bruce's body.

'So the trouble involving Bruce and his activities is now over.'

'That's not the way I wanted this to end, but I guess that confrontation has been a long time coming, and perhaps it might be good for everyone to know the truth.' Skelton sighed. 'But I'll sure miss the gold, and Prospect Town will suffer.'

Kingsley shook his head. 'I doubt it. Creighton Frost's discovery fuelled interest in this place for nearly twenty years. Once word gets out about Bruce Russell's success it'll probably fuel another twenty years of interest. As this is the right area to look, gold will surely get found again. If not, people will still come. This time Hard Ridge won't benefit and Prospect Town will.'

Kingsley's theory made Skelton's eyes open wide as he considered the possibilities.

'Prospect Town *will* grow,' he declared. 'Now that the secret is out it may even prosper more than it did before.'

With that positive thought Skelton set about organizing his men to ferry the bodies down the slope to the pass. Kingsley and Manville stood back to let him deal with the situation, and they remained quiet until Thorndike and Norwell sidled closer.

'So Bruce knew where to find gold?' Thorndike said in a casual manner that didn't show any sign that this was the first non-antagonistic comment he'd ever said to him.

'He knew the area, but it took him years to find anything,' Kingsley said.

'But he found enough to help Skelton build up Prospect Town from nothing.'

'He did, and I'm sure that fact will excite many people.' Kingsley smiled when he noticed Thorndike's smirk, which showed it had already done that. 'Before long they'll be here, so if you want to search you'll need to start looking straightaway for the place where Bruce has been digging.'

Thorndike nodded, and with Norwell he turned away to look over the area. When they headed towards the shelter, Manville sighed.

'I'm pleased you made your peace with Thorndike,' he said. 'But I'm surprised you helped him.'

Kingsley winked. 'I was simply encouraging him so he'd stay here and not annoy me in Prospect Town.'

Manville laughed, but then his face became serious.

'Does that mean you'll definitely be staying?'

'I wasted seven years of my life because of what happened here. Maybe if I take this opportunity for a fresh start, that time won't have been a complete waste.'

'I came to Prospect Valley because of what happened here, too. I got most of the answers I wanted, but I reckon I'll achieve a whole heap more if I make a proper life for myself.'

'Agreed,' Kingsley said. He moved to head on, but then stopped and faced Manville. 'Whatever I end up doing, I won't ever come to this pass again or waste another moment of my life worrying about gold.'

'On that we can both agree,' Manville said. Then he glanced at the line of bodies. Skelton's men were doubling up to move them, and with Thorndike and Norwell turning their thoughts to looking for gold, several bodies including Bruce's had yet to be moved.

Kingsley frowned. 'I'd guess we can also both agree that Bruce got what he deserved.'

'I'm not so sure. I didn't learn the full facts about what happened between Bruce and my father, but my father probably cheated him so I can understand why he got angry.'

'No matter what the truth, Bruce took a big risk when he took on Vandyke, so he died helping us to defeat Friedmann.'

Manville sighed. 'He did, but I'm not sure whether that's enough for me to forgive him.'

'It is for me.' Kingsley took a step towards Bruce's body, and then stopped. 'I reckon I should be the one to take his body back to town, but I could do with some help.'

For long moments Manville looked at Bruce's body before turning to Kingsley. He nodded, and the two men moved forwards.

'Bruce probably found more gold here than my father did,' Manville said as he took hold of Bruce's legs. 'In the end I hope he found something more important: his dignity.'

Kingsley raised Bruce's shoulders. 'I reckon he did.'

They picked up the body and carried it away. When they reached the edge of the slope, raised voices sounded behind them as Thorndike and Norwell started arguing about something.

Kingsley and Manville smiled at each other and headed on down into the pass.